The Heart of the Clan

The Heart
of the Clan

Barbara Cartland

Thorndike Press • Chivers Press
Thorndike, Maine USA   Bath, England

This Large Print edition is published by Thorndike Press, USA and by Chivers Press, England.

Published in 2000 in the U.S. by arrangement with International Book Marketing Ltd.

Published in 2000 in the U.K. by arrangement with Cartland Promotions Ltd.

U.S. Hardcover   0-7862-2484-3   (Romance Series Edition)
U.K. Hardcover   0-7540-4135-2   (Chivers Large Print)
U.K. Softcover   0-7540-4136-0   (Camden Large Print)

The text of this Large Print edition is unabridged.
Other aspects of the book may vary from the original edition.

Set in 16 pt. Plantin by Rick Gundberg.

Printed in the United States on permanent paper.

British Library Cataloguing-in-Publication Data available

Library of Congress Cataloging-in-Publication Data

Cartland, Barbara, 1902–
    The heart of the clan / Barbara Cartland.
       p.   cm.
    ISBN 0-7862-2484-3 (lg. print : hc : alk. paper)
    1. Scotland — Fiction. 2. Large type books. I. Title.
PR6005.A765 H4   2000
    823′.912—dc21
                                              00-021195

Author's Note

George IV's visit to Scotland in 1822 was a triumphant success. His Majesty wore full Highland dress in the Royal Stewart tartan.

The King left London in the *Royal George* on August 1th and four days later in pouring rain at about two o'clock in the afternoon the anchor was dropped off Leith.

He stayed outside Edinburgh at Dalkeith Palace with the sixteen-year-old Duke of Buccleuch and showed remarkable zest for a man of sixty for the Drawing-Rooms, the Levees and the Balls.

"Marriage by Declaration" before witnesses, or Irregular Marriage, was legal in Scotland until the Act was repealed in 1949.

1

1822

The horses reached the top of a steep incline and came to a halt.

The footman jumped down from the box and opening the carriage door said:

"Th' coachman says us must wait here for a while t' give th' horses a rest an', if ye be interested, there's a very fine view, sir."

"Oh, I must see that!" a young voice exclaimed. "Do let us get out, Papa."

The gentleman to whom she was speaking had his foot up on the smaller seat in the carriage, and answered:

"Leave the door open so that I can see it from here. I am too tired to move!"

"It has been a long journey," his daughter said with a sigh, "but we are nearly there."

"That be right, Miss Sona," the footman said. "Th' coachman says it be only 'nother four miles afore we reach th' Castle."

Sona smiled at him as she stepped from the carriage.

Higman was their own servant who had come with them from the south to valet her father and also to act as footman when it was necessary.

The carriage, a very grand one with the Ducal coat-of-arms on its doors, had been waiting for them as soon as they crossed the border.

The journey from Derbyshire had taken three weeks, but they had travelled in very easy stages because Colonel Alister McCarron's foot was paining him owing to a touch of gout that was always worse in bad weather when he could not take as much exercise as he liked.

But now the blustery windy spring was over and Sona was sure that he would soon be walking easily and without pain.

In the meantime as far as she was concerned nothing could be more exciting than an unexpected journey to Scotland with the chance of meeting her relatives and the members of the Clan of which she had heard so much ever since she was a child.

Fiercely proud and staunchly loyal to his Scottish forebears, Colonel McCarron had always resented having to live in England.

But his wife, whom he had adored, had been English, and when she died he had been left with an attractive manor house and a small estate in Derbyshire which she had been given by her father.

It was not only sentiment that made him continue to live there with his only child, but also financial necessity. But he had never forgotten where he really belonged.

When the invitation had come from the Duke of Invercarron for them to attend the wedding of his eldest son, the Marquis of Inver, Sona thought she had never known her father so happy.

"It will be a gathering of the whole Clan!" he had said triumphantly. "Then, my dearest, you will understand what I have tried to explain to you in words, but which can only really be understood when one sees with one's eyes or listens with one's heart."

"You are being quite poetical, Papa!" Sona teased.

At the same time she knew how much being united with his own kith and kin would mean to her father.

They had made hectic preparations to go north, and for the Colonel this meant getting out his full Regimental dress of the Highland Brigade in which he had served.

For Sona it was frantically trying both to buy and to make enough new gowns so that she would not feel ashamed of her appearance when she met her relatives for the first time.

Although she had never seen them she knew a great deal about them.

The Duke of Invercarron was now in his late sixties, and still the autocratic and greatly admired Chieftain of the McCarrons.

They had served him, her father told her, with the loyalty and almost childlike obedience that good Scottish Chieftains evoked in their followers. But they also feared him, and the Colonel had said:

"It is difficult to explain to you, having been brought up in England, what the Chieftain of a Clan means in Scotland."

"You have always made him sound, Papa, as if he was more than a King and a little less than God."

Her father had laughed, but he had answered warningly:

"That is not the sort of thing, my dearest, you should say when we reach Invercarron Castle."

Sona's eyes twinkled and there was a dimple on each side of her mouth as she replied:

"I promise you, Papa, I will not shame you. I will be demure and modest, just the type of maiden you pretend I ought to be."

"What do you mean by that?" her father inquired.

Sona laughed.

"Because although you say one thing, you think another."

Her father did not reply and she went on:

"Mama, as you well know, was high-spirited, impetuous and always an exciting person to be with. I hope that I am like her."

It was the Colonel's turn to laugh as he pulled his daughter to him.

"You are very like your mother, my dear, but in the Castle you must behave as they will expect of you, that is that all women shall naturally be subservient to their men-folk."

Sona had teased him for being an overbearing tyrant all the way to Scotland.

But now as she stepped out of the carriage and saw beneath them a view so beautiful that it took her breath away, she felt that the greatness and the majesty of it must be something like the Chieftain who was waiting for them.

They had been travelling along the east coast and now the sea was blindingly blue as it ran inland into a narrow but deep estuary.

The heather was not yet in bloom, but there were patches of golden gorse and the green of the fir trees was a vivid contrast to the barren bareness of the hilltops.

It was quite different from any country Sona had seen before, and she felt as if something within her responded to its beauty and made her a part of it.

11

She walked away from the carriage hardly aware she was doing so, but entranced by the loveliness of her surroundings.

Finally she sat down on the edge of a peat-hag with the land falling steeply in front of her, some hundreds of feet down to a very narrow strip of pasture land which bordered the sea.

She was so intent on her feelings and thoughts that she started when a man's voice said:

"I knew you would stop here to appreciate the beauty of our land!"

She turned her head sharply and found a man standing beside her who was, she thought, almost as good-looking as the scenery which had held her entranced.

He was wearing the kilt of the McCarron tartan with a bonnet on the side of his head which carried the McCarron crest, and she thought that if this was one of her relatives he was certainly very attractive.

As if he read her thoughts the stranger said:

"Let me introduce myself. I am Torquil McCarron! When I heard you were coming I was determined to have the first glimpse of you!"

"That may have been mere curiosity, at the same time it was kind of you," Sona replied. "I am feeling rather frightened of all those waiting for my father and me at the Castle."

"I see no reason for you to feel that."

As Torquil McCarron spoke he sat down beside her.

"Do you know who I am?" Sona asked.

"Yes, of course," he replied. "Everybody knows what guests are arriving and where they come from and needless to say there has been talk of nothing else since the wedding was announced."

"That is understandable," Sona smiled. "My father and I also were very excited when we received our invitations."

"His Grace is determined to make it a memorable occasion," Torquil McCarron said. "It is certainly a triumph as far as he is concerned."

"A triumph for the Duke?" Sona asked.

She was puzzled not only by what Torquil McCarron had said, but also by a note in his voice that was, she thought, one of bitterness.

"Yes, for the Duke! The Marquis has no wish to be wed."

"Then why did he agree if he feels like that?"

Torquil McCarron laughed, and it was not the sound of humour.

"I see you do not understand the authority of a Chieftain when he chooses to use it."

"Oh, but I do!" Sona contradicted. "My fa-

13

ther has explained to me over and over again that a Chieftain is the father of his people, and just as they follow him in battle to their death, so in life they obey him implicitly."

Torquil McCarron nodded his handsome head.

"That is true, but it is difficult for people who do not live in Scotland to understand that any recalcitrant sons are finally brought to heel."

Again there was that bitter note in his voice and after a moment's silence Sona said a little shyly:

"If what you say is . . . true I am . . . sorry for the . . . Marquis. I have always thought it must be horrible to . . . marry anybody unless it was for love."

"Love!" Torquil McCarron ejaculated. "It is not a question of love where the Marquis is concerned. I do not suppose he has ever loved anybody except himself."

"Then why . . . ?" Sona began.

"What he minds," Torquil McCarron interrupted, "is leaving London, and having to come back to live among us 'barbarians'."

The word seemed almost to vibrate as he spoke and involuntarily Sona murmured:

"Oh . . . no!"

"It is true," Torquil McCarron said positively. "He despises us because he has had all

14

the advantages. Can you not understand? The future Duke had to be educated at Eton and Oxford! The future Duke is presented at St James's! The future Duke must be constantly in attendance upon the King!"

It was quite obvious to Sona from the way he spoke that the man sitting beside her was very jealous.

Once again, as if he knew what she was thinking, he said:

"I am speaking not only for myself, but for those like me who have not had such advantages, but have had to make the best of what is provided for us here in our own small Kingdom."

"And has that not been . . . enough?" Sona asked softly.

"The answer is 'no!' Yet at the same time it would be tolerable if the Marquis were a man like his father, if he loved his people, if the land for which our forebears fought and died meant anything more to him than a source of income to dissipate in the south."

There was so much feeling in Torquil's voice that Sona could not help being moved by what he said.

There was silence. Then she asked:

"May I inquire if we are . . . related, and what is your . . . position in the . . . Castle?"

"My position?"

Torquil McCarron repeated the words almost derisively.

"I am of very little importance. My father was first cousin to the Duke, so I suppose I am second cousin to the Marquis, but of little, if any, consequence in his eyes."

"But you are still a McCarron, as I am," Sona said.

He smiled at her and the darkness went from his face.

"And could I ask for more?" he inquired. "We are related by blood and are part of the history of generations which nobody can take from us."

"No, of course not," Sona agreed.

She hesitated, then she added a little tentatively:

"Perhaps . . . when the Marquis is . . . married he will settle down and . . . love this land as obviously you . . . love it."

She thought Torquil McCarron would contradict her, but instead he said:

"I can see, Sona, for I am sure I can call you that, that you want this to be a fairy story where everything ends happily."

"Of course I do," Sona agreed, "and I want my visit here to be as beautiful as the view I am looking at, at this moment."

"Then that is what we must try to make it," Torquil said. "I hope to see you later."

16

He rose to his feet and as he did so, she saw Higman was beckoning to her from the side of the carriage further up the hill and she rose too.

"Will you come and meet my father?" she asked.

"Perhaps I may have that privilege another time," Torquil McCarron said. "I think now you should be on your way without delay."

"Yes . . . of course," Sona agreed.

It would be a mistake, she thought, to arrive later at the Castle than they expected.

Quickly she started to walk over the heather back to the carriage and only when she had a short distance to go did she find to her surprise that Torquil McCarron had left her and was moving away in the opposite direction so quickly that he was already out of ear-shot.

She reached the carriage and when the horses set off again she said to her father:

"I expect you saw me talking to a young man, and a very handsome one."

"Who was he?" her father inquired, "and why did he not come to meet me?"

"I asked him to do so, but he said it might delay our arrival at the Castle."

"Did he tell you his name?"

"Yes. It was Torquil McCarron, and he said his father was a first cousin of the Duke."

Her father frowned for a moment as he concentrated, then he said:

"I have a suspicion of who he is, and if I am not mistaken, he is one of the family skeletons in the cupboard."

"Oh, no, Papa! How could he be?"

"I will find out for certain before I say any more."

"Now you have made me curious," Sona remarked, "and he seemed to be very resentful of the Marquis."

"What did he say?"

Her father's voice was sharp.

"He said the Marquis, having had all the advantages of an English education, prefers to live with his friends in London rather than with his Clan in Scotland. Is that right, Papa?"

Her father hesitated and Sona knew he was choosing his words.

"As you know," he said at length, "I have not been back to Scotland since I married your mother, but nevertheless I have been in touch with many of my relatives and I have met Napier Inver in London."

"You have met him!" Sona exclaimed. "What is he like?"

Again there was a perceptible pause before her father replied:

"Rather a strange young man, and with a will of his own which I can understand would inevitably clash with his father's."

"You mean they do not get on?"

Colonel McCarron nodded.

"From all I have heard they fought continually until Napier went south to spend his time with the Bucks and Beaux who surrounded the Regent."

"Is there anything wrong in that?" Sona inquired.

"A Scotsman would tell you there is a great deal wrong with any man who would prefer the south to his native land."

The Colonel paused before he added:

"At the same time I understand that it is largely due to the Marquis that the King intends to visit Scotland this year."

"That will be wonderful for the Scots."

"I suppose so," the Colonel conceded and shut his eyes, as if he was determined the conversation should come to an end.

Driving along the narrow roads which twisted between pine trees and over stone bridges which spanned streams running in cascades down the mountain sides, Sona puzzled over the bitterness in Torquil McCarron's condemnation of the Marquis.

She told herself, however, that it was obvious any young man who could not enjoy the same privileges was bound to be envious.

Before, when her father had talked of the

Duke whom he greatly admired and of his son, Sona had always thought of the Marquis as a Prince Charming with a background so romantic, so exciting that it meant more to her than any of the fairy tales on which she had been brought up.

The battles in which the McCarrons had been victorious, the legends which were part of their history, had been told and retold ever since she was a small child until she felt she could not bear that anything should spoil the wonder and glory of it all.

Because a wedding was always exciting she had told herself that the Marquis had fallen in love with some beautiful Scottish girl and that their marriage would be another romantic story which to Sona was more poignant than anything she could read in a book.

She was already aware that the bride, whose father was the Earl of Borabol, owned land which marched with that of the McCarrons'.

"An eminently sensible match," her father had said when the invitations arrived. "The Clans will stand shoulder to shoulder and support each other."

It occurred to Sona that perhaps it was too obvious an alliance to be anything but of convenience.

As the Marquis was always in England it was unlikely that he would have become so enamoured of the daughter of the neighbouring Chieftain that he would wish to marry her.

In which case, the marriage must have been arranged by the Duke and the Earl with the bride and bridegroom having little say in the matter.

Then, because the idea depressed her, she told herself that this was nonsense.

Of course, the Marquis, a grown man thirty-two years of age, would not be forced into doing anything he did not wish to do, whatever his father might say.

If he wanted to marry, why should he not court a bride amongst the beautiful and desirable women, who, if gossip was to be believed, were found in abundance at Carlton House and now that the King had moved, at Buckingham Palace?

It was stupid, Sona thought, but Torquil McCarron had upset her, and now she was worrying about what she would find at Invercarron Castle instead of looking forward to it excitedly and perhaps childishly as she had been doing.

As the horses drew them down to sea level and they crossed the bridge over the inlet of the sea, there was a straight road ahead and at the end of it Sona had her first glimpse of the Castle.

It was exactly as she had thought it would

be, with turrets and towers gleaming white against a background of dark fir trees, and it stood high above the sea on one side and with the moors rising steeply behind it.

It was so beautiful in the gold of the setting sun that Sona forgot all the doubts that Torquil McCarron had aroused in her and felt it was just as she had imagined a dream Castle for a dream Prince and Princess who were to be married and live happily ever after.

Then as the Castle vanished amongst the trees she quickly tidied her hair, tied the ribbons of her bonnet and shook out the skirts of her travelling gown.

Her father still kept his eyes shut but she was certain he knew where they were.

"We will arrive in a few minutes, Papa," she said warningly.

"Thank God for that!" the Colonel exclaimed. "I loathe these long journeys! One thing I shall insist on, Sona, is that we have a good rest before we return home."

"I am sure the Duke will be delighted to keep us for as long as we wish to stay," Sona replied.

"I only hope so," her father said dryly. "He is an unpredictable man, so be careful you do not say anything to upset him."

"I will be very careful, Papa."

As Sona spoke the horses turned in through huge iron gates flanked on each side by lodges with castellated roofs.

There was an avenue of ancient trees and at the end of them she could see the Castle again and felt her heart begin to beat quickly.

"This is an adventure," she told herself, "and there is no reason to be afraid! After all, I am a McCarron!"

At the same time, when they were received by kilted attendants and found themselves in an impressive Hall decorated with stags' heads, Sona was aware that perhaps for the first time in her life she felt nervous.

She had never been shy, having helped her mother entertain her father's friends ever since she had been a small girl.

Perhaps it was the atmosphere of the Castle that seemed overwhelmingly large, or perhaps it was Torquil McCarron's depressing words, but as they followed the kilted retainer up the wide stone stairs which led to the first floor Sona wanted to hold on to her father.

He was certainly looking very impressive, wearing his kilt which he had donned as soon as they crossed the border between England and Scotland, his plaid held on his shoulder with the huge brooch set with a Cairngorm and his sporran swinging as he moved.

In a way he seemed different from the father with whom she was so familiar either in

23

his uniform or in the riding clothes he usually wore at home, when he was alone with her in the small rooms which could be packed, she thought, into a corner of the Castle and hardly be noticed.

They reached the first floor and the servant paused for a moment before he pulled open two huge polished mahogany doors.

They went into what Sona knew was the Chieftain's Room which her father had often described to her when he told her about the Castle.

It was even larger and more impressive than she had expected it to be, and because there were quite a number of people present she felt their faces seemed to swim before her as a servant announced:

"Colonel Alister McCarron, Your Grace, and Miss Sona McCarron!"

Then they were moving forward to where at the far end seated on a chair that seemed almost like a throne was an elderly man, and as they drew nearer to him Sona thought he looked like an eagle.

There was the same imperious air about him, the same searching scrutiny in his eyes, and if the eagle was King of the Birds, the Duke in his own way was just as royal.

The Duke held out his hand and she noticed that her father bowed before he took it.

"It is good to see you, Alister!" the Duke said.

"How are you, Iain?" her father replied.

"I am well enough to see that this wedding proceeds according to plan," the Duke replied.

Then his eyes were on Sona.

She curtsied and he said:

"You are like your mother."

But it was not a compliment.

The other people in the room were men dressed like her father, and Sona guessed they were all relatives of some sort or another.

Then she was taken to her bedroom which seemed to her to be a mile down a high passage.

It overlooked the gardens which lay below the Castle and beyond them was the sea sweeping into a crescent-shaped bay.

The evening sunlight glittering on the smooth water was as beautiful as the flower-filled gardens with the fountain playing in the centre of them.

"It is all so lovely!" Sona exclaimed involuntarily, and the Housekeeper smiled.

"That's what we want ye to think, Miss Sona, on yer first visit. I ken yer mither weel — a bonny lady she were. Ye must miss her."

"I do," Sona agreed. "I wish she could be here with us today. I expect you are very excited about the wedding."

"It is what His Grace has wished for," the Housekeeper said briefly, and Sona wondered that she had no more to say.

By the time her clothes were unpacked it was time for dinner and because she felt it was important to make a good impression, she put on one of the prettiest gowns she had brought with her.

She was glad she had done so, for when she reached the Chieftain's Room she found the other women staying in the Castle were elaborately dressed in the latest fashion and covered with jewels.

Sona soon gathered that those who had already arrived in the Castle were the McCarrons who lived in the south and had been asked a day or two ahead of those who lived in Scotland, so that they could rest before the ceremonies.

Being a family of great importance and extremely wealthy, the McCarrons had made, Sona was to learn, brilliant social marriages.

Because they could pick and choose they had also married beautiful women and Sona, looking around, thought it would be impossible to find anywhere a party which contained finer looking men or lovelier ladies.

Certainly the evening dress of the men was a perfect foil for the silk gowns and the diamonds which glittered on white skins, or in the case of one beautiful woman with red hair, glowing green emeralds.

The Duke was not present and Sona learned that the Marquis would be their host at dinner.

"Iain, I'm afraid, is in poor health and it is going to be a severe trial of his strength if he takes part in all the festivities which have been planned for this wedding," she heard one of the older members of the party say to her father.

"The Duke is certainly making it a big event," the Colonel replied.

"It is — to him!" was the answer. "It has taken him nearly five years to make his son see sense, and now, as he said to me yesterday, Napier has only capitulated because he is almost on his death-bed!"

"He sounds a somewhat reluctant bridegroom," Colonel McCarron remarked.

"Of course he is, and who shall blame him?" was the answer.

Sona was hoping that more would be said, but at that moment the door in the Chieftain's Room opened and a man came in who she knew instinctively was the Marquis.

Never had she imagined anybody could look so regal, so overpowering, and at the same time so disagreeable.

The Marquis was dark, and if his hair was black as a crow's wing so were his eyes.

He was scowling and his mouth was set in a hard line. Although his lips smiled when he greeted the new arrivals, it did not change the expression of his eyes.

He spoke to several people before he reached her father.

"How are you, Colonel?" he said, holding out his hand.

"Very glad to have arrived here safely! I do not think you have met my daughter, Sona."

Sona curtsied, feeling again unaccountably shy.

"No, we have not met before," the Marquis said.

She put her hand into his and as she touched him she felt what she could only describe as a strange vibration.

She did not know if it was a good or a bad one, she only knew there was something vital about him; something which made her know that he was vividly alive as perhaps few other people were.

Then he passed on to speak to somebody else and she felt she must have imagined it.

They went into dinner in the huge Banqueting Hall with portraits of the McCarrons on the walls and ancient weapons arranged in a pattern over the carved fireplace.

The silver on the table was all of artistic and historic interest, but Sona had eyes only for the Marquis, who seated at the end of the table seemed in a way even more majestic than his father had been.

His chair was carved and ornamented with the arms of the McCarrons like a throne, and the light glinted on the crested buttons of his black velvet coat and on the jewel embedded in the lace of his cravat.

He looked exactly as she had wanted him to look, except for the expression on his face.

It seemed impossible that any man could look so angry — or was it resentful? — while he apparently talked quite pleasantly to the ladies on his right and on his left.

They were doing their best to entertain him, and it was obvious that one of them who was young and extremely beautiful was endeavouring coquettishly to dispel the darkness that seemed to envelop him, but without avail.

The food was delicious. There was fresh salmon from the river in which Sona knew her father would be longing to fish as soon as he was able to walk without pain, haggis and other Scottish dishes, as well as great joints of beef and saddles of young lamb.

Course succeeded course.

Then finally there were the sweet high

notes of the pipes and the Duke's personal piper swung round the table, playing the tunes which Sona had heard from her cradle and which all through the centuries had led the McCarrons into battle.

Because she was moved by the pipes and because they more than anything else gave the party the fairy-tale atmosphere she had hoped for, she found herself listening to them and at the same time looking at the Marquis, almost as if she expected him to feel as she was feeling.

He was not speaking, but staring at the glass of wine he held in his right hand.

Then suddenly, almost as if she had willed him by the intensity of her gaze, he raised his eyes and looked into hers.

It took her by surprise, since she had been watching him almost as if he was not human, but rather a creature of her imagination, and she was momentarily startled.

Then as their eyes met she felt as if they spoke down the length of the table, but what he said and what she heard was not clear.

Then the pipes ceased and the spell was broken.

The next morning Sona was awakened by the pipes playing beneath her window.

She had already learned from her father

that it was traditional for the pipers to walk around the Castle first thing in the morning, and she lay listening to them and feeling they brought her a magic that she had always longed for, had known was there, and yet had never found.

When finally they died away into the distance she sprang out of bed, drew back the curtains and, without waiting to be called, dressed herself.

It was very early, and she thought few people would be about if she went down into the gardens and found her way to the sea.

Because she had always lived in the heart of Derbyshire she had only seen the sea a few times in her life, so the sea as well as the Castle was an enchantment.

The servants who were cleaning and tidying looked surprised at her appearance, but she bade them "good morning", and walked through a door which led her first on to a terrace, then down a long stretch of stone steps into the garden where the fountain was playing. The dew was still on the grass and there was the fragrance of flowers as she walked along small gravel paths until she found her way through a wooden gate and onto some grassland which led to a sandy beach.

There was a faint mist over the sea and the blue of the sky was reflected in the blue of the water as it lapped over the rocks covered in seaweed.

There was salt in the air, and Sona felt it was all part of the beauty which had been hers ever since she had reached Scotland.

Then she saw a small boat that appeared to be approaching a wooden jetty which jutted out a little further along the shore.

Because she was interested she walked towards it, and when she reached the jetty the boat was much nearer and she could see who was pulling the oars.

Somehow it was not surprising but seemed inevitable that it should be Torquil McCarron.

He brought the boat alongside the jetty, shipped his oars, and tying the boat competently to one of the wooden struts climbed out to stand beside her.

"Good morning, Sona!"

"Good morning!" she answered. "What have you been doing?"

"I have been inspecting my lobster-pots," he replied, "and was also hoping to see you."

She smiled at him.

"I cannot believe that you were expecting me to be up so early."

"Why not?" he asked. "You are a country girl and only the lazy, pampered beauties from London lie in bed until the sun has risen."

"You certainly cannot accuse me of that!"

"I have no wish to accuse you of anything."

He was looking exceedingly handsome, she thought, bare-headed, his eyes very blue against the sunburnt skin of his face.

Without thinking about it they walked to the end of the jetty.

There was a wooden seat against the wall that bordered the garden on which they sat down, and Torquil turned sideways to look at Sona before he said:

"Well?"

"Well . . . what?"

"What do you think now that you have seen the Duke, and of course, his son?"

"I think they both are charming," Sona replied defiantly.

Torquil laughed.

"It is what I might have expected you to say, but I prefer to hear the truth."

"It is the truth!"

"Then shall I say, because you are obviously extremely intelligent, that I want a more perceptive answer."

"Very well," Sona replied. "I think the Duke looks exactly as a Chieftain should and yet at the same time somewhat frightening."

"And his son?"

"I have been . . . wondering why he is so . . . unhappy."

33

"I told you the reason."

"That he wants to live in England after he is married? Surely he can do that until his father dies?"

"I doubt if that is possible when his wife's roots are here. And one thing is quite certain, she would not like London."

"How do you know?"

"I know her."

"Then if they are so incompatible," Sona said, "surely it would be best if they did not marry?"

Torquil laughed.

"You should say that to the Duke! He is obsessed with the idea that the Clans should be united, as they were in the dim ages."

"Were they? That is interesting."

"The Borabol Clan broke away from the McCarrons centuries ago and it has been a thorn in our flesh ever since. Ask your father."

"I will, but I doubt if he is aware of it, or I would have heard about it before."

"You must study our history while you are here, Sona. You will find there are many twists and turns amongst the Clans, and a McCarron who is determined always gets his own way!"

"At the expense of other people, I presume?"

"Of course! They are unimportant."

34

Sona hesitated for a moment. Then she said:

"Why are you so concerned by this marriage? What does it mean to you?"

There was a perceptible pause before Torquil said in a very different voice:

"It means nothing to me, of course — except as one of the Clan."

The way he spoke did not ring true and after a moment Sona said insistently:

"I think you have your own reasons for disliking the fact that the Marquis is marrying."

Again Torquil laughed.

"Now you are being imaginative! It is just that I think it a mistake for the future Chieftain of our Clan to be unhappy and distressed by being united with a wife he does not want and who has been forced on him by his father. But, of course, it is really none of my business."

Now Sona was quite sure he was speaking for effect and knew that what he was saying was not true and he was making excuses.

It suddenly struck her that perhaps he was in love with the bride-to-be and that was the reason why he disapproved of the marriage so much.

"Is she very beautiful?" she asked and it was obvious to whom she was referring.

"Wait until you see her," Torquil replied.

"She is coming to the Castle for dinner."

"Will you be there too? I expected to see you last night."

"Did you notice my absence?"

"Of course I did! Where were you?"

"At home."

"And where is home?"

"About a mile away from the Castle."

"I hope you will show it to me one day," Sona said, "but you have not answered my question. Will you be coming to dinner?"

Torquil looked around and rose to his feet.

"I am not!" he said in answer to her question. "And if you wish to remain friends with me, as I hope you will, I suggest you do not mention my name."

"Why not?"

"There are reasons," he replied darkly, "reasons which I have no wish to explain to you. Instead I only ask you, if you will, to trust me and be my friend."

She looked up at him uncertainly and he said:

"It is something I want very much! In fact, more than I dare to say at this moment."

Now there was a deep note in his voice which made her look quickly away from him.

"I think I must go back to the Castle," she said. "It must be nearly time for breakfast."

"We shall meet again!" Torquil said firmly.

36

He took her hand in his as he spoke and raised it to his lips.

As she felt his mouth on her skin it gave her a strange feeling which was not what she expected.

Then because she suddenly felt it was somewhat reprehensible of her to be there alone, talking to a man she had met only yesterday, she turned towards the garden gate and passed through it before he had time to open it for her.

Without looking back Sona walked quickly along the gravel path towards the steps which led back to the terrace.

2

After breakfast the gentlemen all left to fish in the salmon river which ran through the valley behind the Castle.

The Colonel went there in a pony-cart, determined if he could manage it to walk down to the river and fish for as long as his leg would allow it.

There was no sign of the ladies from London who had breakfast in their rooms, and in fact the only other woman present besides Sona was an elderly cousin who ate her porridge in a disapproving silence, sprinkling salt on it in the correct Scottish manner.

Sona was amused to see that the gentlemen all ate their porridge standing which her father had told her was traditional.

"The oatmeal which was the Scots' staple diet," he explained, "is always eaten standing so that they are on the alert and ready for any enemy who might appear when they were without weapons in their hands."

It was difficult in the Baronial Dining-Room, with silver on the table and gold-framed portraits looking down from the walls, to think that there might be rival Clans creeping through the heather, or foreign enemies like the Vikings approaching from the sea.

But Sona already knew from the tales her father had told her and from what she had read of the history of the McCarrons that they had had continually to expect attack both by land and by sea.

The bay in front of the Castle had been a convenient place for the Vikings to beach their ships, and seeing the number of fair-haired, blue-eyed retainers amongst those who waited on the Duke, she thought they had left behind them when they departed more than memories of pillage and rape.

It struck her that Torquil with his colouring and height looked more like a Scandinavian than a Scotsman, and she seemed to recall her father saying that the Picts who had manned the fort, the remains of which were to be found on all the moors in this part of Scotland, had been small, dark and wiry little men.

There was, however, nothing that resembled a Viking in the appearance of the Marquis except perhaps his height, and although she expected to see him at breakfast, he had not appeared.

After the other guests had left the Castle and the elderly cousin had gone presumably to her own room, Sona found herself alone.

She decided this was a good opportunity to explore, and as nobody had suggested she might be interested in viewing the Castle, she thought she could take it upon herself to look around.

She inspected the pictures, the stags' heads, the ancient shields and claymores that had been used by her ancestors.

Then she wandered past the Chieftain's Room to a Drawing Room which was filled with French furniture which surprised her until she remembered how closely at the time of Mary Queen of Scots Scotland had been connected with France.

Further down the corridor a large mahogany door was slightly ajar and peeping through it she saw a Library.

This was something she had somehow not expected because although her father was an avid reader he had never mentioned there was a Library at the Castle.

It was a high room with tall windows that overlooked the garden, as did her bedroom, and she stood for a moment looking out over the bay wondering if she would see Torquil in his boat.

She was curious about him because there

was obviously some mystery that he had not yet explained to her, and it was something that she felt existed inside as well as outside the Castle.

Last night after dinner the ladies were all whispering together in a surreptitious manner which told Sona they did not wish to be overheard and she had therefore moved away from them to look at some miniatures that were displayed in a cabinet at the far end of the room.

None the less, she had wondered what they were saying and was quite sure it concerned the Marquis.

It would be difficult for anybody, even a stranger like herself, not to be curious about him, and she knew that the elegant and beautiful women from London were doing everything they could to beguile him out of his bad temper.

They obviously knew him very well, and because they all bore important titles, Sona was certain they had belonged, before the King came to the throne, to what had been referred to as the fast "Carlton House Set".

Even in the wilds of Derbyshire she had heard people talking of the excesses and immorality of the friends of the Prince Regent and of the contrast between his life and that of the dull, old-fashioned Court at Buckingham

Palace where the King was often so deranged that he was kept in a strait-jacket.

She had wondered what the brilliant social figures said and did.

She knew of course that Lord Byron, after his disastrous marriage, had to flee from England, and that Beau Brummel, once the leader of the Social World, was in exile in Calais.

She had heard of the new King's infatuations for various women, most of whom were older than himself.

The scraps of gossip that reached Derbyshire left her curious but ignorant and without any real conception of what life in London could be like.

She found herself thinking that she was very dull and countryfied compared to the ladies with their rouged faces, red lips and hair dressed in styles she had never seen before.

It was not surprising that they more or less ignored her, and when the gentlemen came from the Dining-Room and everybody else seemed on such familiar terms she had felt very much an outsider.

She had gone to her father's side and after a moment he said:

"I imagine, my dear, you are thinking I should go to bed early, after such a long journey."

"It would be a sensible thing to do, Papa."

"Then as I am tired, I will, for tonight at any rate, do what you think is the right thing."

"Perhaps we could slip away, Papa, without anybody noticing us."

Her father smiled at her.

"I think that would be the tactful thing to do. It would be a mistake to break up the party."

Nobody appeared to notice as they walked together towards the door and only as they passed through it did Sona look back and realise that in fact one person was aware they were leaving, and that was the Marquis.

She had gone to bed thinking about him, and now in the Library, although the books were an irresistible interest, she found herself thinking of him again.

He must have loved the Castle when he was young.

How could any boy not want to bathe in the sea, row his own boat in the bay, shoot over the moors, and catch salmon in his own river?

She understood now why her father had always spoken of Scotland as being a Paradise where a man was concerned, and it seemed extraordinary that with so much to entertain him here the Marquis should prefer London.

Sona looked at the shelf in front of her and found a history of the McCarrons, and as she

43

turned over the pages she found herself thinking that the Marquis also would be familiar with the tales of bravery that she had listened to ever since she could remember.

"Why do I keep thinking of him?" she asked and put the book back onto the shelf.

As she did so she heard the door of the Library open and turned her head to see the Marquis come into the room.

It was almost as if thinking of him had conjured him up.

She could not help noticing how well his kilt became him, and that he looked even more elegant in it than any Englishman would look in the white breeches and cut-away coat which with highly polished Hessian boots had become almost a uniform. The Marquis was so deeply concentrated on his own thoughts that he did not notice Sona until he reached the desk in the centre of the Library.

Then as she moved slightly he started and his dark eyes were on her face.

There was a perceptible pause before he said:

"Good morning! You are an early riser!"

She knew intuitively that he was not referring to the time of day it was now but that he must have seen her much earlier in the morning passing through the garden towards the sea.

"There is so much to see and I do not wish to miss a second of it," she replied.

She thought his lips twisted a little despite the fact that he still appeared to be glowering, and there was a distinct frown between his eyes.

"I understand from what your father said last night that this is your first visit to Scotland," he remarked.

"Yes, the first, and therefore you can understand how thrilled I am to realise it is even more beautiful than I expected."

As she spoke Sona moved a little nearer to him but she was looking towards the window as she went on:

"I cannot believe that there is any place more lovely in the whole world, and I am half afraid I shall wake up and find I have been dreaming!"

As she spoke it suddenly struck her that considering the way the Marquis was feeling about Scotland she was being unnecessarily provocative.

She glanced at him and as if he realised what she was thinking he said:

"I too thought like that many years ago."

"But not now?" Sona asked involuntarily.

"As you say, not now."

"But it is yours — your country, your home, your people, our blood! Surely that

45

means something to you?"

As she spoke she was surprised by her own daring, but with her father she had become so used to expressing her feelings candidly that the words had just come to her lips without her considering the implication of them.

There was silence for a moment. Then the Marquis said:

"I see you are absurdly romantic!"

He spoke somewhat rudely and Sona replied quickly:

"There is nothing absurd in being proud of being a McCarron!"

"You have been indoctrinated," the Marquis remarked slowly, "with the same traditional balderdash that has been drummed into me ever since I was a child."

"And is there any harm in that?"

Now because she realised he was deliberately challenging her, Sona felt her temper rising, and her anger made her reckless.

Why should he be so disagreeable, and why should he wish to disparage that which to any other man would be a joy beyond words?

She did not look at him but walked close to the open window to stand with her hands on the ledge feeling the soft breeze on her cheeks.

"It is very easy for you," she said, "when you own so much, to belittle and disparage it. But have you ever thought what this Castle stands for in the hearts of those who have not had your advantages and are as it were in exile in other parts of the world?"

The Marquis did not reply and after a moment she went on:

"I can tell you what it means to my father, who through no fault of his own lives in England which has always been in a way alien to him because it is not Scotland."

She turned to look at the Marquis to see that he was listening. Then went on:

"To him the Clan is a rock to which he clings because it is the one thing to which he wholly belongs. It keeps him from feeling that he is ever alone, insignificant or unimportant. He is a McCarron, and wherever he may be, in the sands of darkest Africa or the heat of India, he is still one with the family of which he is a part."

Sona spoke passionately and before the Marquis could reply she added:

"And that is what every McCarron feels wherever he may be, and the stability of it all depends on one man — the Chieftain!"

Her voice seemed to throb on the air. Then there was silence.

She did not turn her head again. She merely waited, and after a moment the Marquis said:

"Yes, the Chieftain. A totem-pole to which the natives must bow subserviently and obey.

I only hope, Sona McCarron, that you will stay here long enough to learn the truth, and of course enjoy the Poop-Show for which you have come!"

The Marquis spoke so scathingly that Sona drew in her breath. Then she heard the Library door slam and realised she was alone.

For a moment she could hardly believe she had had such an interchange of words with the Marquis.

Then as the blood burned in her cheeks she knew how reprehensible it had been and how badly she had behaved.

She should not have spoken to him so openly and because she had done so he had every right to answer back although she had not expected it to be so harsh or so upsetting.

'Now he will be angry with me,' she thought.

Then she ceased to think of herself, but of him. What had happened?

Why was he so unhappy, so bitter? And was Torquil right in thinking that what he deeply resented was having to leave his life of gaiety in London for one of responsibility in Scotland?

"I should not have spoken to him in such a manner," she chided herself.

Then she felt that he should not have replied in the same way.

Because she felt agitated she went out of the house, and fearing that the Marquis might see her moving through the gardens as he had this morning she walked instead a little way up the drive.

Then she saw a ride leading through the woods which encircled the back of the Castle, as it were a jewel in a green setting.

She moved through the trees feeling as if the scent of them somehow soothed her troubled mind.

She walked for quite some way and was out of sight of anybody passing along the drive when she had the feeling that she was not alone.

There was somebody near, and although she could not see him she was unmistakably aware that she was being watched.

It made her feel uncomfortable and it was creepy.

Then as she walked on, determined she would not be afraid, Torquil McCarron came from between the trees just ahead of her.

For a moment it was a delight to see him again. Then it turned to one of surprise.

"What are you doing here?" she asked. "You always seem to pop up in the most unexpected places!"

"To meet by the sea or in the woods is

hardly unexpected in Scotland," he replied. "We will probably meet next on the moors."

Sona laughed, and somehow it was a relief after the dramatics she had encountered with the Marquis.

"Why are you walking in the woods?" she inquired.

"I was taking a look round," he answered vaguely, "and hoping that perhaps you might join me."

"Why should you expect me to do anything of the sort?"

"If you are 'fey' as you should be, then you would have known that I was calling for you."

Sona looked at him in a rather startled manner. Then she told herself he was speaking lightly and she replied:

"I did not hear you. I merely came for a walk."

"Because you wished to get away from the Castle!"

"Why should you think that?"

"I know the Castle, and you are beginning to feel that it overwhelms you and you are stifled and afraid."

He spoke in a way that made her want to shudder.

"That is not true," she said. "I am enjoying myself more than I can ever say, and I do not want anything to spoil my happiness."

"That I would not want to do," Torquil said. "At the same time not everybody is as happy as you are."

Inevitably Sona thought of the Marquis. Then she realised that Torquil was speaking of himself.

"Why are you so unhappy?" she asked.

"It is a long story," he said. "Do you want to hear it?"

"Of course, if you really wish to tell me your troubles."

"Let us find somewhere where we can sit down," he suggested.

He started to walk along the narrow, moss-covered path which led further into the wood.

It struck Sona as she followed him that if anybody knew she had met Torquil this morning and was meeting him again so quickly they might consider it very strange and per-haps reprehensible.

Then she told herself that nobody was likely to be in the least interested in what she was doing and, after all, he was a McCarron and a very handsome young man.

It was certainly more interesting and more amusing to be with him than to be snarled at by the Marquis.

Torquil led the way to a little clearing where there were trees which had been blown down in a gale and cut up by the woodmen. A fallen tree-trunk provided a seat which he indicated with his hand.

Sona sat down, aware that the sunshine coming through the tree-tops was warm on her bare head, and for the first time she wondered if it would be expected that she should wear a bonnet when she left the Castle.

She was so used to running impulsively into the garden at home that it had never struck her she should dress herself more circumspectly for a walk in the Castle grounds.

As if once again he knew what she was thinking Torquil said:

"You are looking very lovely, but then dozens of men must have told you that."

She smiled and shook her head.

"Then Englishmen must be blind!"

"The Scots are supposed to be dour," Sona replied.

"Only when it comes to money," Torquil answered, "and as I have not any, my words instead must be golden."

Now Sona laughed and it was a sound that seemed to mingle with the song of the birds in the trees.

Torquil drew off his bonnet and she thought looking at him that his very fair hair was definitely inherited from some Norse ancestor, and his blue eyes against his sun-tanned skin made him look very much the hero of one of her fairy stories.

"Tell me about yourself," she said. "There is so much that I do not understand about you, and about the other McCarrons for that matter."

"That is not surprising," Torquil replied, "and yet as we are all part of the same blood, we should be able to understand each other."

"Yes, of course."

"If I were the Marquis, do you know what I would do?" he asked.

She looked at him inquiringly.

"I should ask you to marry me! We would reign together at the Castle and make it a place of gaiety and happiness where we could look after our people and they would respect and obey us as their beloved Chieftain and his wife."

As he spoke Torquil's voice was almost hypnotic but it seemed to Sona as if he was describing not just a fancy of his mind, but a dream that came from his very soul.

Because she felt embarrassed by what he had said she replied lightly:

"If wishes were horses, beggars would ride, and although you have told me very little about yourself I feel that we are both beggars enjoying the crumbs from the rich man's table."

She thought he would laugh, but instead he said:

"I do not want the crumbs. I want to sit at the head of the table!"

The way he spoke made Sona feel nervously that he was intending to be bitter, as the Marquis had been, but in a different way.

"Personally," she said getting up from the tree trunk as she spoke, "I am very content with things as they are. I am in Scotland for the first time, I am staying in a wonderful Castle, and you have been kind and friendly towards me."

"And what about me?" Torquil asked.

Although Sona had risen he was still seated on the trunk of the tree.

"Perhaps you are asking too much," she suggested. "We all have to be content with what we have."

"Why?"

"Because that is the way of the world. Some people have, and some have not. We just have to accept the position in which we are born."

"That is something which I have no intention of doing," Torquil said sharply.

Sona walked two steps away from him and stood irresolute, wondering why he did not move and thinking it a pity that their conversation had changed from being light and amusing.

As if he felt her indecision he said:

"There is no point in your waiting for me. I

am not allowed in the 'Holy of Holies' — the Castle of my ancestors!

"Go back to Napier Inver and ask him how much he is going to enjoy his wedding, and tell all those other stuck-up McCarrons who are fawning on him that one day I will surprise them. One day they will find I am a force to be reckoned with!"

He seemed to be speaking rather wildly, but there was an underlying violence and determination in his voice that made the words ring out in the quietness of the wood.

"I . . . do not . . . understand," Sona said.

"You will!" he replied, and swinging his legs over the trunk of the tree he walked away in the opposite direction.

She stood staring after him until she could no longer hear him moving through the low branches, his feet cracking the dry leaves that had fallen the previous winter.

Sona gave a little sigh.

The McCarrons were an uncontrolled, over-dramatic lot, and their behaviour was something she had never expected.

She wondered if she would ever be able to understand either the Marquis or Torquil.

Then she told herself that only her father, being a McCarron, would be able to explain what was happening.

Slowly she retraced her steps along the nar-

55

row path which led back to the drive.

'One thing is certain,' she thought, 'I certainly seem to upset my relatives in one way or another.'

Because she could not think of what else she could do, she went back to the Castle and found several more McCarrons had arrived to stay for the wedding.

They had come from Edinburgh and Perth, and being Scottish were very unlike those who had come from London.

The women were quietly dressed, their faces bare of cosmetics, and they spoke in low, refined voices.

The men concerned themselves with talking about sport and making enquiries as to how many salmon had been caught the previous week.

After Sona had introduced herself she soon became aware that they thought it was a pity that her mother had been English. They did not actually say so in words, but it was obvious they thought a Scot could find happiness only with one of his own kind.

"I am so looking forward to this wedding," one of the elderly women said to another. "I was desperately afraid that dear Napier would find himself lured into marriage in the south, and that, you know, would never do!"

"No, indeed!" the other lady agreed. "The

wife of a Chieftain must be somebody who understands our ways, and who could be more appropriate than Jeannie?"

"I have never met her," the first lady replied, "but the Countess is a woman who I am told has brought her family up to understand their duty."

They sounded, Sona thought irrepressibly, very dull.

Only as the ladies went into luncheon did she learn for the first time that the bride-to-be was arriving that evening for a large dinner party that was to be given so that all the relatives staying in the Castle could meet her.

It would certainly, Sona thought, be something of an ordeal, for after luncheon was finished there hardly seemed to be a moment when some new arrival was not announced by a kilted man-servant.

There were McCarrons who had come from the Western Isles and others from the Orkneys and Shetlands.

There were McCarrons who had travelled from the Lowlands, and others who lived quite nearby in the Highlands.

Sona reckoned that there must be fifty relatives staying in the Castle, and she thought that if she were the bride she would find it a distinct ordeal to know that they were all inspecting her and deciding in their own minds if she was good enough for the Marquis.

The Earl, the Countess and their daughter did not arrive until after it was time to dress for dinner, and the maid who helped Sona into her gown told her they were in the Castle.

"What does she look like, Maggie?" Sona inquired.

"A proper Scots lassie, miss," Maggie replied.

It was not a very adequate description, and Sona realised she would just have to wait and see for herself.

She found it difficult not to keep thinking of Torquil and wondering not only what he was doing but why he was barred from the Castle.

He was so good-looking and obviously well educated, and it seemed extraordinary if he lived so near and was a McCarron that he should not be invited to the dinner.

She was determined to find out sooner or later the reason for his absence, but as it might entail explaining how she had got to know him in the first place, she knew she would have to wait her opportunity and not evoke uncomfortable questions.

'I suppose it was wrong of me to be alone with him in the woods,' she thought, 'but it did not seem so, and certainly nobody has taken any trouble to entertain me.'

She supposed the Marquis was still angry

with her, and when he had not appeared she learned from some casual remark that he had gone to join the fishers on the river. Neither was there any sign of the Duke.

"I suppose our Chieftain is keeping himself on ice until this evening," she heard one of the beauties from London say in a frivolous tone.

"I cannot say I miss him!" another one replied. "He always makes me feel as if I have a spot on my nose and a stocking falling down!"

"You are lucky," the first beauty laughed. "My husband literally shakes when the Duke speaks to him, and you would think we were living in the days when the Chieftain had the power of life and death over his Clan."

"That is the truth where Napier is concerned," the other lady replied in a low voice and they both laughed.

Sona thought that nobody would notice what she looked like, at the same time, woman-like she wished to look her best.

She chose what she thought was the most spectacular gown amongst those she had brought with her from England, but was well aware as she did so that it looked very plain and dull beside the gowns worn by the London beauties.

Nevertheless, when she looked in the mirror after Maggie had buttoned her into it, she would have been very foolish if she did not know that with her mother's grey eyes and her hair which had a touch of gold and red in it, she looked very pretty.

Her gown was white, as was suitable, and it was trimmed around the hem with ruchings of tulle in which nestled small bunches of musk roses.

There were roses outlining the tulle at the top of her *décolletage,* and she wore a little bunch of them in the curls on the top of her head.

"You ought to be the bride, Miss Sona!" Maggie said in what seemed like awe-struck tones. "That's what you ought to be!"

"There will be time enough for that," a voice said at the door as the Housekeeper came into the room. "I hope ye are all right, miss. I've hardly had time to see ye because I've been run off me feet. There's bells ringing like clarions with every lady wanting something at the same time!"

"It must be a lot of work for you," Sona said sympathetically. "At the same time it is exciting, is it not?"

"It is for us as is not really a part o' it," the Housekeeper replied rather enigmatically.

The Colonel met Sona at her door and she walked with her father down the passage towards the Chieftain's Room.

"Enjoying yourself, my dear?" he inquired.

"Very much, Papa."

"Our relatives have all been saying such nice things about you," the Colonel said, "which has made me very proud."

"I am doing my best not to disgrace you," Sona replied.

"So I should hope," the Colonel answered smiling. "Remember, some old busy-body will be watching you like a hawk, even though they tell you they are too blind to see anything."

Sona chuckled with laughter and slipped her arm through her father's, squeezing it as she did so.

"I love you, Papa!" she said, "and I know it has put you in a good temper that you caught a salmon."

"Only a small one," her father admitted, "but it was satisfactory to know I have not lost my skill."

"Of course you have not," Sona said.

They reached the Chieftain's Room from which came the chatter of voices.

As they entered Sona saw the Duke was seated, as he had been the night they arrived, in the throne-like chair.

He was looking magnificent with decorations on his velvet jacket, and the silver on his sporran was almost dazzling.

Sona once again thought he looked like a

great eagle, and she was certain that his eyes missed nothing of what was going on around him.

She and her father walked to greet him and as she curtsied to him he said sharply:

"I hear you have been talking with that scallywag who calls himself Torquil McCarron!"

At his words Sona felt the blood rising in her cheeks and knew she was blushing.

"He introduced himself to me on our journey here," she said.

"I am sure he did!" the Duke answered. "Pushing young swine! You are to have nothing to do with him, do you understand?"

It was a command given in a voice, Sona thought, as if to a raw recruit who had just joined the regiment.

She bowed her head but did not speak, and was relieved when the Duke's attention was distracted by some new guests he had not previously met.

As her father moved away she walked beside him to speak to one of the men with whom he had been fishing earlier in the day.

Now she found herself thinking that Torquil certainly had reason to be bitter and resentful if that was the way he was treated.

Why should the Duke speak of him in that manner? And why should she be ordered to ignore him?

If the McCarrons wanted to be rude to each other, she thought, and there was nobody to stop them, that was no reason why she should be treated like a schoolgirl who did not know her own mind.

It was then as she looked back towards the Duke that she realised that the Marquis was standing a little way to the side of him, and she wondered if he had overheard the conversation his father had had with her and what he had thought about it.

He was looking as magnificent as he had the night before, but he was scowling and appearing, if possible, to be more disagreeable than ever.

His lips were turned down at the corners, there was a frown on his forehead, and his eyes seemed so dark as to be almost expressionless.

"What is wrong with him?" Sona asked.

As if in answer to her question the door opened and a servant announced:

"The Earl and Countess of Borabol and Lady Jean McBora!"

The room seemed suddenly silent as everybody turned their heads towards the newcomers, and Sona was alert with interest.

The Earl of Borabol was a thick-set, weather-beaten looking man without much presence, although he carried himself proudly.

His wife was stout with a complexion that had obviously suffered from the weather. The diamonds which blazed on her chest and in her grey hair were no compensation for the black, uninteresting gown she wore which made her appear old-fashioned and almost shabby.

Their daughter was behind them and it was therefore impossible at first for Sona to see her, until her father and mother had almost reached the Duke.

Then as she looked at the bride-to-be it was difficult not to give an audible gasp.

Lady Jean was a strapping young woman who obviously would always look out of place in a Ball Room or in evening dress.

Her face was redder than her mother's, and while her arms were white her hands were burned deep brown from the sun.

She had the pale red hair characteristic of so many Scots, which was dressed in an untidy bun at the back of her head, and her eyelashes, which were the same colour, gave her a ferrety look which was extremely unattractive.

One glance was enough to tell Sona why the Marquis hated the marriage, and she asked herself so intensely that she almost said it aloud:

"Why in that case has he weakened and

been forced into it?"

No handsome man, she thought, would ever voluntarily wish to marry a young woman who looked like Lady Jean, and for a man who was used to the fascinating, witty beauties of London it could only be purgatory that would be impossible to contemplate.

"Why? Why must he do this?" Sona wanted to ask, and looked at the Marquis.

As she did so she realised he was not looking at Lady Jean, who was now speaking to the Duke, but across the room at her.

3

When she got to bed Sona lay in the darkness thinking of the evening and feeling it was one of the strangest she had ever spent.

The shock when first the Duke had commanded her not to see Torquil again was overshadowed by the appearance of the bride-to-be and her sudden sympathy for the Marquis.

She had felt before that she almost hated him for his rudeness to her and for everything that Torquil had told her about him.

Now she knew she would not wish her worst enemy to have to marry somebody as unattractive as Lady Jean.

All through dinner the bride-to-be sat looking dull and rather sulky, and making little effort to respond to the Duke.

She was sitting on his right and, watching them up the table, Sona could see that he was trying in his own way to be pleasant and to put his future daughter-in-law in a good light to the other guests.

Although she did not hear exactly what was said Sona was certain that Lady Jean was answering her host in monosyllables, and after a while the Duke gave up trying and sat looking merely fierce and more like an eagle than ever.

The Marquis also hardly said a word to his future wife, and confined his conversation to his dinner partner on his other side, a very attractive lady from London who was a McCarron by birth and had married one of the gentlemen-in-waiting to the King.

Sona had already admired her a great deal, and she thought now that as she raised her eyes to the Marquis and pouted at him with her red lips, the contrast between her and the girl who was to become his wife was too poignant to be anything but embarrassing.

Because Sona realised that she was neglecting her own dinner partners she turned to the man next to her to ask:

"Do tell me about the McBora Clan. I am afraid I know nothing about them."

"Then you cannot have studied our history very closely," her partner replied. "The McBora's have been a thorn in our flesh for generations, after being formed by a McCarron who had a quarrel with the Chieftain of the time in much the same way, I imagine, and for much the same reasons, as Napier is at logger-heads with his father today."

"And what was the reason?" Sona asked.

The McCarron to whom she was speaking glanced a little apprehensively up the table at the Duke, almost as if he was afraid their conversation would be overheard.

Then he answered in a low voice:

"My sympathy is all with Napier. Our host, to say the least of it, can be very difficult and overbearing."

Looking at the Duke Sona was sure that was true.

Then she asked in a voice that was little above a whisper:

"I suppose the Duke has insisted on his marrying Lady Jean."

"Of course," her informant answered, "although 'tricked' him into it would be the better word."

Then as if he felt he had been indiscreet he started to ask Sona about her own life and her home in the south.

"It was bad luck your father having to be away for so long," he remarked. "I have seldom found a McCarron who is happy unless he is surrounded by his own people."

"My father was very happy with my mother," Sona asserted.

"Now that she is no longer with you," her

dinner partner replied, "I hope Alister will come back and live here."

Sona looked startled.

It was something she had never envisaged and she was not certain it was what she wanted personally.

She loved Scotland, and it was certainly the most beautiful place she could imagine.

At the same time, although she had been at the Castle such a very short time, she wondered if all the contentions, dramatics and mysteries would not make it uncomfortable if one had to endure them for ever.

In Derbyshire she hunted with her father in the winter and accompanied him when he went shooting, and there was always a lot for her to do locally although in retrospect it seemed somewhat trivial.

Yet she had to admit that she had never seen her father look so happy for a long time as he had since they arrived at the Castle.

She could see him now across the table talking animatedly to a pretty, not so young lady, who was listening to him attentively with a smile, and it suddenly struck her that one day he might wish to marry again.

This was something else she had never contemplated before, but he was still an active man and outstandingly handsome. She felt she should face the fact that while the ladies of

London showed not the slightest interest in her, they looked at her father flirtatiously and he seemed very much at home in their company.

"If Papa married again what would become of me?" Sona asked herself.

Although since she was eighteen she had been to quite a lot of parties at home with their neighbours and had met a number of young men who had paid her compliments and were eager to dance with her at the Hunt Balls or on other occasions, she had not received a proposal of marriage.

She wondered now if it was only because the men in question were not particularly eligible or whether she was not attractive enough for anybody to wish to spend the rest of his life with her.

It was a depressing thought which inevitably lowered her spirits. Then the McCarron on her other side said:

"May I tell you, you are looking very beautiful, Sona? And that I think it is rather tactless of you."

"Tactless?"

"Well, should I say it is somewhat unfair to the young woman sitting next to the Duke?"

It was difficult for Sona to know what to reply, but an answer was obviously expected and after a moment she said:

"Perhaps somebody could suggest to Lady

Jean how she could improve her appearance."

"I think you would need a magic wand to do that!" her dinner partner replied dryly.

Because she felt sorry for the girl and also sorry for the Marquis, when dinner was over Sona deliberately went up to Lady Jean and introduced herself.

"I am Sona McCarron," she said, "and I am so grateful to you."

"Grateful to me?" Lady Jean inquired.

She had a dull, uninteresting voice, and when she talked she fluttered her pale eyelashes shyly which made her look more ferrety than ever.

"It is because of your wedding that I have come to Scotland for the first time," Sona explained.

"So you live in the south?"

"Yes. My mother was English."

Lady Jean did not reply for a moment. Then she said:

"My father does not approve of us Scots marrying Sassenachs!"

She spoke almost aggressively and Sona felt her hackles rise.

"My father fell in love with my mother the first time he saw her," she said, "and they were very happy together."

"My marriage is for the good of the Clan," Lady Jean answered, "and because of it there

71

will be no more warring between the McBoras and the McCarrons."

"Surely 'warring', as you call it, is something that happened only in the past?" Sona questioned. "And perhaps now that the King is coming to Edinburgh, the Scots and the English will in the future be more friendly."

Lady Jean's eyelashes seemed to flutter even more violently.

"The English are cruel to us! They always have been!" she exclaimed. "Scotland should be an independent kingdom, as is our right!"

Now there was no doubt that she was being aggressive, and Sona would have answered her back if she had not told herself that it would be a great mistake to become embroiled in a political discussion. She must try, instead to help Lady Jean as a woman.

"Tell me about your trousseau," she said beguilingly. "Are you having your gowns made in Edinburgh?"

"Certainly not!" Lady Jean said sharply. "There are excellent seamstresses amongst the women of the Clan. We also have weavers and lacemakers, so any money that is expended by my father will benefit our own people."

It sounded very laudable.

At the same time looking at the ugly brown that Lady Jean was wearing, Sona thought that her clothes would certainly not please the

Marquis who was used to seeing women dressed in fashions which originated in France.

"Tell me about your wedding gown," she begged.

"My wedding gown," Lady Jean answered, "was worn by my mother, my grandmother and my great-grandmother. It is an heirloom which I revere, and which I shall pass on in my turn to my daughter and granddaughter."

"You have not told me what material it is made in," Sona persisted.

"It is trimmed with bobbin lace, with the McBora crest incorporated in the design," Lady Jean replied, "and it is mounted on hand-wove wool which comes from our own sheep."

She spoke so proudly that Sona, who had been thinking that any wedding gown must be made of the finest silk or of Brussels lace, could not imagine what Lady Jean could look like, except that it would be impossible for it not to be bulky and undoubtedly unbecoming.

She made, however, just one last effort.

"If I can help you in any way before your wedding, Lady Jean," she said, "I hope you will not hesitate to ask me to do so. After all, we must be nearly the same age, while everybody else here seems somewhat older."

She forced herself to smile as she spoke, but Lady Jean's lips were turned downwards and she looked across the room to where her mother was sitting.

"I have Mama to help me," she replied, "and of course my own relatives will be coming to the wedding."

She walked away as she spoke, her feet thumping in her flat, sensible slippers and the large steps she took made her look as if she was striding over the moors rather than on the Aubusson carpet in the French Drawing-Room.

Sona gave a little sigh.

She had done her best and if she had failed it was certainly not her fault.

Because she felt uncomfortable standing alone she moved towards two of the ladies from London who were seated together on a sofa.

As she drew nearer to them she heard one of them say to the other:

"My heart bleeds to think of him having to kiss a creature like that after Madelaine."

The other lady laughed. Then she said:

"Madelaine only said *'au revoir'* when Napier left her — she was so certain he would be back. And having seen the bride, I am only wondering whether it will be before the honeymoon or after."

Now both ladies were laughing and because in some way she did not understand what they said hurt her, Sona moved to the other end of the Drawing-Room where there was an open door.

It led into what she had already learned was known as the "Card Room".

There were several green-baize tables laid ready for those who wished to play chess or card games, and she thought that the McCarrons who lived in Scotland and doubtless the McBoras would disapprove.

But for the moment the room was empty and she occupied herself in looking at the pictures which were French like those in the Drawing-Room. She found one painted in soft tones of blues and pinks which she was sure was a Fragonard.

She was staring at it when she heard the deep notes of the voices of the gentlemen in the Drawing-Room and knew that they had joined the ladies.

She supposed she should go back, and yet she was reluctant to do so.

She felt she could not bear to listen to any more of the sniggers from the sophisticated McCarrons or see the Marquis looking so disagreeable.

It spoiled everything she wanted to feel about the Castle, and she wished that instead of being here at this moment she could be transported back to the days when the McCarrons were warring either with other Clans or against the English.

She was sure then they had something more important to talk about than the wedding of two people who were completely and absolutely unsuited to each other.

While she was still looking at the picture in front of her two gentlemen came into the room.

"Come and play piquet with me," one of them said to the other. "I find it depressing to be surrounded by nothing but McCarrons. I am afraid to open my mouth in case I say something indiscreet."

"I agree with you," the other said, "and Harry has said the same thing. As soon as this damned wedding is over we will go back to London, and I assure you it will be a long time before I come north again!"

Listening, Sona realized that both were men who had married McCarrons.

Neither of them were wearing kilts and they looked very slim and smart in their evening clothes, with their white shirts and intricately tied cravats.

She found herself wondering what the Marquis would look like if he was not in Highland dress, and she was certain there would be an elegance about him that would make him outstanding even in Buckingham Palace.

She had walked to the furthermost end of the room and because she did not wish to be noticed she sat down in an armchair which had its back to the card tables.

She was no longer able to see the players but she could hear them and a few seconds later one of them remarked:

"Hello, Napier! Have you come to join us? If so, let us have a game of écarté. I feel like taking some money off you!"

"With my present run of luck, that is something you will undoubtedly do!" the Marquis replied.

He must have sat down at the table and a second or two later one of the men said:

"It is your deal."

"What is the stake?"

"A 'monkey'," the Marquis replied.

"Agreed."

There was silence for a moment. Then the man who had spoken first said:

"George and I were talking about leaving immediately after the wedding. We were hoping that you would come south in time to join my house party for the Derby. I know you are running a horse, and so am I."

"I have every intention of seeing Rollo run," the Marquis said with a hardening of his voice.

"Then I will expect you the night before the meeting," his friend said. "It will be a bachelor party, although that does not of course exclude any 'bit o' muslin' that you wish to accompany you. I have already invited several charmers who I do not think will disappoint my guests."

The other man called George laughed and said:

"The one thing about you, Percy, is you always have an eye for detail."

"I try to," he replied, "and neither Napier nor you have ever criticised my choice of such delights in the past."

"And I am sure I shall not do so in the future," the Marquis said.

Sona was suddenly aware that this was not the sort of conversation to which she should be listening.

She was not so innocent that she was not aware that a "bit o' muslin" was a name for women who were not recognised or spoken to by any lady of quality.

She could also in a way understand why the Marquis had accepted such an invitation immediately after his marriage.

At the same time she was aware how deeply it would shock his Scottish relatives and certainly anger the McBoras.

Apart from knowing what kind of party it

was planned to be, it would certainly be insulting for a bridegroom to leave his bride so soon after they were married.

Having read so much about Scottish history she could visualise only too clearly how another feud could be ignited between the two Clans who ostensibly were being united by the marriage. Now once again they would be at each other's throats.

It was a situation which, because the Scots had long memories and were always thirsty for vengeance, could increase and multiply from one small incident into a vendetta which would continue for generations.

"He should not go," she told herself.

Then she heard the man called Percy say:

"I must tell you of an amusing story at the last house party I gave. I invited the most delectable little Cyprian . . ."

The way he was speaking made Sona realise that she must make the gentlemen at the card table aware of her presence.

Percy was beginning his story as she pushed her chair back almost roughly and rose to her feet.

The noise she made alerted the three men at the card table and as she stood up she saw their faces turned towards her, an expression of surprise on each one.

She walked towards them.

"I am sorry if I startled you," she said, "but I sat down for a moment and fell asleep. It must be the strong air."

The three men slowly rose to their feet.

"Come and join us," one of them who she thought was Percy, suggested. "If you do not know how to play we will teach you, and let me add for my own part it would be a pleasure!"

Sona smiled at him.

"Thank you, but I think I should go to bed. Perhaps another night you will give me a lesson."

"In anything you wish to learn," Percy replied, "and it is something I shall very much enjoy."

There was an innuendo in his voice which made Sona blush.

Then as she curtsied her eyes met the Marquis's and she felt herself almost recoil at the expression in them.

She could not translate it even to herself, but she felt almost as if she looked into a blazing fire and was burnt by it.

Then she slipped away into the Drawing-Room where the chatter of voices rose like a wave of the sea to sweep over her.

Because sleep eluded her, Sona found herself thinking of the expression in the Marquis's eyes and repeating over and over again the things he had said to her in the Library.

She was just drifting into an uneasy slumber when she thought she heard the sound of a drum.

Then she told herself it was part of a dream or perhaps the beat of her heart and slipped away into unconsciousness.

Sona was awakened by the sound of the pipes and only when she was dressing did she remember the drum of the night before.

"There is a lot of music in Scotland," she said to Maggie who was buttoning up her gown, "the pipes at dinner and again this morning, and very late last night I thought I heard a drum beating beneath my window."

"Nay, miss, ye couldna have!" Maggie exclaimed.

"Why do you say it like that?" Sona inquired.

"Because if ye heard the drums, miss, 'tis a warning!"

"A warning?" Sona asked.

"Somebody in the family will die!"

Sona was silent.

Now she could recall reading among the many legends of the Clans of Scotland that for the McCarrons there was a ghostly drummer who played when somebody of importance in the Clan was about to depart this life.

She had read it in a very old book and as her

father had not mentioned the superstition, she thought it would be something that had long been forgotten.

And yet from the way Maggie had spoken she realised the girl was quite shaken by what she had just said.

"I expect it was my imagination," she said quickly.

"Ye be a McCarron, miss, and they says that many of ye are 'fey', but when there be a death they all hear the drum."

"Then it will be quite easy to ascertain if I was right or wrong," Sona said. "I will find out if anybody else in the Castle heard the drum last night."

There were only three men and two elderly women in the Breakfast Room when she entered it, and as she helped herself to some porridge, taking only a small helping, she said:

"I thought, although I may have been mistaken, that in the middle of the night I heard music of some sort."

For a moment her remark evoked no particular response. Then one of the men replied:

"If you did, it is not surprising. In two days' time both Clans will be gathering round the Castle and the place will be extremely noisy. I expect the locals are already practising so as to out-play their rivals."

"At the last wedding I attended," one of the women said, "the pipes gave me a headache which lasted for nearly a week! One piper is enough in my opinion, but a dozen or two can be agonising!"

The other guests laughed.

"You had better not let the Duke hear you say that. He told me last night that he was extremely proud of his pipers, and he is determined they will march ahead when he and Napier go to the Church and then escort the bride and bridegroom after the wedding back to the Castle where they will be playing for most of the time during the reception."

The lady who complained of a headache gave a groan.

"You can trust Iain always to overdo things," she said tartly, "and I am quite certain Napier does not want all this palaver at what should be a solemn and quiet occasion."

"I agree with you," one of the men said, "and by the way, where is Napier this morning? I understand he was coming fishing with us."

"He breakfasted early to avoid us," another man replied, "and who shall blame him? I too dislike talking first thing in the morning."

This remark forced the rest of the breakfasters into silence and Sona, having finished hers, left the room.

As she did so she saw the Countess of Borabol and Lady Jean coming down the corridor and was glad she had avoided them.

"I will go for a walk up on the moors," she decided.

She went to her bedroom and put on a pair of sensible walking shoes.

It was a warm day and she thought if she was walking she would not want a shawl over her thin gown, and she decided although it might seem unconventional that she would not wear a bonnet.

"Nobody will see me," she told herself.

Yet she wondered if she might run into Torquil.

At least it would be somebody pleasant to talk to if he was not being bitter and envious of the Marquis, and it would be easier than conversing with her relatives.

She slipped down a side staircase, which she knew would take her to the ground floor, to avoid meeting anybody else who was going to the Breakfast Room.

Then as she moved along the corridor which led to the garden she walked straight into the Marquis.

He came out of a room which she saw as the door opened was an office, and he looked surprised to see her.

"I am going for a walk," she said, feeling she must explain why she was there.

"Alone?" he asked.

"I understand all the men are going fishing," she replied.

"And the women are not likely to be as energetic as you are," he smiled. "Where are you going?"

She had the feeling he was trying to be pleasant to make up for the way he had behaved the last time they had been alone.

"I thought I would go up on the moors."

"A good idea!" he said. "If you go straight up the drive you will see the beginning of a path opposite the gate. Follow it and it will take you to a cairn from which there is a magnificent view."

Sona smiled.

"That is just what I wanted to find."

"When you have finished admiring the scenery," the Marquis went on, "you can bear north through some rather thick heather, and you will come to a cascade. There is a small path, although it does not show itself, across the top of it by which you can come down on the other side. It is my favourite walk."

"Thank you. Thank you very much!" Sona said. "It sounds very exciting."

"Well, enjoy yourself! That is what I would

like you to do while you are here."

"Thank you," Sona said again.

There was a pause while she felt there was something she wanted to say, although she was not certain what it was, and she had the feeling that he felt the same.

Because for no reason she could ascertain she was shy, she gave him a little smile and went on down the corridor.

She had the curious feeling that he was watching her go, but she forced herself not to look back. When she reached the great brass-studded door it was open and she went out into the sunshine.

She walked up the drive feeling as if she was escaping from something which as Torquil had said was overpowering, and when she reached the lodge gates with their crenellated tops, she turned to look at the Castle.

With its towers and turrets it was very fairy-like, and she thought it would look even better when she reached the cairn which the Marquis had described to her.

It was easy to find the path opposite the front gates, and she followed it over some low ground which was thick with heather and almost immediately began to climb.

It was quite a stiff walk of over half a mile going uphill all the time until ahead she could see a small cairn.

She was hot and a little breathless by the time she reached it, and as she threw herself down on the mossy ground beside it she saw the Marquis had not exaggerated when he had told her there was a magnificent view.

Below her, looking almost like a child's toy or something out of a dream, was the Castle with the Duke's standard flying from the tower.

Beyond was the sea and the land jutting out crestlike around the bay. Then, far in the distance, silhouetted against the horizon was another part of Scotland.

It was enchanting in the morning sun and everything was quiet and still. All she could hear were the bees in the heather, the cry of the gulls and occasionally the call of a grouse flying low over the moor.

She sat there for a long time feeling as if Scotland itself spoke to her and especially this the land of her fathers.

"This is part of me, part of my blood and of every breath I draw," she told herself.

She tried to forget for the moment the personal dramas taking place in the Castle, and to see it as she had before she came to Scotland, filled with McCarrons who had fought violently and died heroically, and had loved every inch of their land and all it meant to them.

But even while she was lost in a dream-world of her own it was somehow not surprising to find she was no longer alone.

Torquil came from behind the cairn and sat down beside her.

"I told you we would meet next on the moors," he said.

"It is so beautiful!" Sona breathed.

"And so are you!"

It was something she had not expected him to say and she looked at him in surprise.

"I have been thinking about you, and you have haunted me ever since you arrived."

"I thought you were haunted by too many other things to include me!" Sona said lightly.

"I think you are the solution to all my problems," he said. "Will you marry me?"

For a moment Sona thought he must be joking, and as she looked at him with startled eyes he said:

"I mean it. You are the loveliest person I have ever seen, you are a McCarron, and what more could any man ask?"

As he spoke he took her hand in his and raised it to his lips.

Astonished and bewildered for a moment Sona did not know what to say.

Yet when she felt the touch of his lips on her skin it made her feel that she did not wish him to say any more, and she did not want him to touch her.

She took her hand away.

"Say you will marry me," Torquil pleaded. "I love you, and I have a plan to which I hope you will agree."

"What . . . plan?"

It was difficult to speak for her heart was beating in an uncomfortable manner.

She was not certain whether it was excitement or agitation at what had happened so unexpectedly.

"As you very likely know," Torquil said, "one can be married by Declaration."

Sona did not answer and he explained:

"It is the law that if two people say they are man and wife in front of witnesses, then they are married!"

He waited and after a moment reluctantly, feeling as if she spoke from a very long distance, Sona asked:

"What . . . are you . . . suggesting?"

"I am suggesting, my beautiful Sona, that we are married by Declaration and we will announce that we are man and wife to your relatives."

Sona looked at him incredulously.

"Are you . . . serious?"

"Of course I am serious," he answered. "What would be the point of saying we are merely engaged and expecting the Duke to arrange another marriage immediately on top of the one he has planned for his son?"

He paused before he went on almost as if he was saying aloud what had been in his mind:

"By the day after tomorrow the whole Clan will be here, the grander members of it staying in the Castle, the rest encamped in the grounds. That will be the moment when we will announce that we are married, and there will be nothing anyone can do but congratulate us."

He spoke with a note in his voice that sounded to Sona like one of triumph and she said quickly:

"No . . . of course . . . not! I could . . . never do anything like . . . that!"

"Why not?"

"Because it would upset my father, and the Duke has told me not to speak to you."

"How did he know we had done so?" Torquil asked sharply, then added before she could reply:

"But of course — everything that happens is reported to the Chieftain and I might have guessed that wherever we were there would be eyes to see and ears to hear."

Sona gave a little gasp.

"You mean we can be seen here at this moment?"

Torquil shrugged his shoulders.

"More than likely. In which case they will run and tell the Chieftain."

"I must not upset him deliberately after what he said," Sona cried. "I must make it clear that it was not my intention to meet you here."

"Why should you be afraid of him?" Torquil asked. "When the wedding is over you can go south, but I want you to stay, Sona. I will make you very happy, and everything will be different once you are my wife."

There was a little pause before Sona asked:

"What do you mean . . . different?"

She was trying to think clearly because Torquil had surprised her and her mind felt as if it was packed with cotton-wool.

"We will be together, and I will make you very happy," he said.

She knew as he spoke that was not the proper answer to her question, but because it was difficult to make him keep to the point she replied:

"Although I am very . . . honoured that you should ask me to be your wife, we have only just . . . met and I have not yet . . . introduced you to my . . . father."

Torquil moved a little nearer to her.

"Let us do it after we are married. Think what fun it will be, a real adventure! You will be married in a different way from other girls, and it will be so easy, so simple, with none of the fuss and commotion of a wedding which nobody enjoys."

"That is not true," Sona said, "I think I should enjoy my wedding . . . if I was marrying . . . somebody I . . . loved."

"I will make you love me."

She shook her head.

"I do not think love is like that. I think love happens and one cannot do anything about it. It is suddenly there and one recognises it because it is . . . overwhelming and . . . irresistible."

"That is what I will make you feel."

Sona smiled.

"When I do I will . . . marry you. Until then my answer must be no!"

"How can you be so dull, so stuffy, so like the McBoras?"

Sona laughed as if she could not help it.

"How can you say I am like the McBoras?"

"To me you are as beautiful as any Venus worshipped by the Romans."

Now there was a depth in Torquil's voice which told her he was being sincere and truthful, and because she did not wish to hurt him Sona said:

"Thank you for being so . . . kind to me."

"I do not want to be kind, I want to make

love to you and to teach you to love me."

He would have moved nearer still, but she put out her hands in a defensive gesture.

"No . . . please."

"Why not? I want to kiss you."

"No, you must . . . not do . . . that."

"Why not?"

"Because it is all too . . . soon . . . too quick. I want to have . . . time to . . . think."

"You are to think about being married, but not about being kissed."

He would have put his arms around her, but Sona pushed him away.

"Please . . . Torquil, you are not to . . . frighten me."

"You are being infuriating!" he exclaimed. "I thought you were one of the adventurous McCarrons, that you would enjoy being different, and dare to defy the pomposity of the old guard."

Sona gave a little sigh.

"I do not want to . . . defy anybody. I just want to be . . . happy."

"By making me miserably unhappy?"

"I have no wish to do that."

"It is what you are doing. I want you! If we were married it would be very wonderful, I promise you."

"If we were to marry," Sona said, "it would not be in a 'hole-and-corner' fashion . . . but with my father's . . . consent and, if we are here . . . the Duke's."

Torquil laughed, and it was an ugly sound.

"So we get back to the Chieftain and you know already that he would say no. If you are not allowed to speak to me, you would certainly not be allowed to marry me."

"He would not stop me if I loved you," Sona said, "and if Papa agreed to our marriage."

"How can you be so obtuse and so cruel?" Torquil asked violently.

Because it was such an unfair accusation it made Sona angry.

"Do you really think it is fair of you," she countered, "when you have met me only two or three times surreptitiously and have made it clear that you are not invited to the Castle, to ask me to marry you in an underhand manner?"

She drew in her breath and went on:

"I have not met your mother and you have not met my father. Surely you must know that would be entirely the wrong way for us to . . . start our . . . married life?"

Torquil made a sound which she was sure was one of exasperation.

"I am trying to explain to you," he said, "that it would make things very much easier."

"For you . . . or for . . . me?"

"For me, in the first place, but also for you. Once we were married everything else would sort itself out. We are both McCarrons, and when they had got over their surprise, I am sure everybody would think it very romantic."

"My father would think it extremely reprehensible," Sona contradicted. "We are very close to each other, especially since my mother died, and he would be deeply hurt and very grieved if I did not trust him to meet the man I wanted to marry until it was too late for him to interfere."

"As he would do!" Torquil said bitterly.

He sat for a moment staring blankly at the view below them. Then he said:

"I did not imagine you would be like this. The best thing you can do is to go back to the Castle and tell Napier that you agree with him that the McCarrons who live here are barbarians and beneath his condescension."

His voice sharpened and he continued:

"I am sure he will want you to commiserate with him for having to marry a McBora who looks more like a fox than a woman and doubtless smells like one!"

As Torquil spoke, spitting out the words, he rose to his feet and started to run through the heather, leaving not by the path along which Sona had come, and which led directly to the Castle, but away to the right where she could see roofs of the village and the spire of the Church.

She watched him go, feeling as he moved swiftly over the rough ground that he would not look back.

Only when he was almost out of sight did Sona realise that her heart was beating uncomfortably in her breast, her lips were dry and she felt as if she had been buffeted by a strong wind, or struggling in a rough sea.

It was like a dream, but it had all happened. Torquil had pleaded with her to marry him with an undeniable charm which had turned to bitterness and anger when she had refused him.

"How could I marry him in such circumstances?" she asked.

She knew now he had gone that she not only had no wish to marry him, but she did not even like him.

He might be incredibly handsome, but she knew instinctively, perhaps with the senses that Maggie had described as 'fey', that there was something wrong about him.

"I must not meet him again," she told herself.

Then because she was half afraid, although it was very unlikely, that he might come back, she rose to her feet and set off to find the cascade which the Marquis had told her about.

She walked for a long time before finally she found it, first by hearing the noise of the water, then coming upon it unexpectedly.

It was a very beautiful cascade, pouring out over heather-covered rocks and falling fifty feet into a deep pool from which the water moved slowly away in a stream which she fancied eventually reached the sea.

It was so lovely that she sat down in the heather and looked at the water glistening iridescent in the sunshine.

It was dark brown with peat, but when it splashed as it reached the basin below, it made her think of the white crested waves that she had always believed were horses for mermaids.

She found herself wanting to read again the fairy stories which had always thrilled her and the legends that came from Scotland and were an indivisible part of her imagination.

Finally, when she began to feel a little hungry, she felt it must be luncheon time and she should return to the Castle.

She rose to climb to the top of the cascade and found as the Marquis had described to her a little sandy path, almost hidden by the high heather on one side of it.

She was just about to walk along it when a rabbit rose almost at her feet and ran ahead of her.

It was obviously frightened and its little white tail bobbed up and down as it shot along the path.

Then unexpectedly in the very centre of it, stopped, and hesitated, then suddenly retraced its steps doubling back past her.

In sheer fear it accelerated its pace and shot past Sona actually grazing her ankle as it did so.

She looked back, but it had disappeared and she thought it was a very strange thing to do.

She was used to seeing rabbits in the woods at home, but she had never known one hesitate on a straight path before, then return the way it had come.

She walked on wondering at its peculiar behaviour.

Then as she reached the exact spot where it had turned she saw there was a roughness to the path where it had been covered with sand and a few faded leaves.

There seemed nothing particular to frighten the rabbit and make it change its course, but because she was curious she bent down to look closer at the ground.

As she did so some of the sand seemed to disappear and with it one or two leaves.

She reached out her hand to scrape away the remains. Then she drew in her breath.

In the centre of the path there was a trap!

Sona had seen animal traps at home and some used in the past that were known as 'man-traps'.

Her father had forbidden the use of any sort of trap in his woods, and the keepers collected any they found and put them in the stables where Sona had seen them before, on her father's instructions, they had been buried.

One of the things about a man-trap that frightened her was its gaping teeth, and she had known that once a man put his foot into it there was no escape and his leg would be so terribly damaged that it would have to be amputated.

Now as she brushed away the sand that was supported on very fine twigs she could see that the trap in the middle was definitely a man-trap and a very dangerous one.

She knelt looking at it with frightened eyes. Then she could hear the Marquis saying very clearly:

"It is my favourite walk."

She could also hear Torquil saying how much the Marquis was hated because he thought of his Clan as 'barbarians'.

Slowly it all seemed to sink into her mind, and as she looked down at the trap she saw how it was set with its jaws wide open for a man's leg, but it was not attached as most traps were so that the man once in it could not escape, but was loose.

Then she was aware there was only some rough grass between the side of the path and the edge of the cascade.

This meant that if the Marquis or anybody else had stepped on the trap and got a foot caught in it, there was every likelihood of the victim falling over the edge of the cascade and into the pool below, where he would have been stunned by the rocks and drowned.

It was so diabolical, but at the same time so clever, that Sona could only drew her breath in horror at what she knew was attempted murder.

Who could have thought of anything so terrifying? And immediately one name came to her mind.

Then resolutely she dismissed this as absurd.

Torquil might be envious, he might even hate the Marquis, but there was no reason to suspect him of being a murderer.

She told herself it was not her job to find out who had done it, but to prevent the crime from taking place.

Carefully and deliberately she cleaned away what was left of the twigs and the leaves which had held the concealing sand.

Anybody now coming along the path would

be able to see the trap quite clearly, but before nightfall somebody must come and remove it.

Then she got to her feet and started to run as quickly as she could back down the way she had come towards the Castle.

4

Only when the Castle came in sight did Sona slow her pace. At the same time she was impelled by an urgency that would not be denied.

She had already decided that the only person she would tell must be the Marquis and she must see him alone.

She was certain it would be a great mistake that anybody else, and especially the Duke, should learn what she had discovered.

She could imagine how the relations would exclaim and snigger over it, and she was convinced it must be a secret between herself and the man for whom it had been intended.

When the great door of the Castle was in sight she saw there was a carriage in front of it and the luggage of some new guests was being unloaded.

As the footmen were all busy it gave her the opportunity to slip past them and to turn down the passage by which she had left the Castle and which led to the secondary staircase.

Only as she reached the office out of which the Marquis had come when she was leaving for her walk did she wonder if perhaps he was inside.

If he was not, it struck her it would be a good place where she could ask to see him and where nobody would overhear what was said.

Because she was in such a hurry she did not stop to knock on the door, but merely turned the handle, and as she opened it she saw with a feeling of indescribable relief that the Marquis was there.

He was sitting at a large desk in the centre of the room with a pile of papers in front of him.

It was then when she had found him and knew she had to search no further that she felt a sudden weakness sweep over her and was aware that she was so breathless at the speed at which she had run that it was impossible to speak.

She could only stand just inside the door, her breath coming in quick gasps, having no idea that with her eyes very wide in her pale face and her hair blown by the wind, she looked very strange.

The Marquis stared at her, then slowly rose to his feet.

"What is the matter, Sona?" he asked. "What has happened?"

It seemed to Sona as if her voice came from a very long distance and it sounded almost incoherent as she replied:

"There . . . is a . . . man-trap . . . waiting to . . . kill you on the . . . path above the . . . cascade!"

She saw an expression of incredulity on the Marquis's face, then everything seemed to be swimming around her and she shut her eyes because she felt dizzy.

The next thing she knew was that somebody was carrying her across the room and the strength of his arms made her feel safe.

She felt herself being set down on what must be a sofa because her legs were raised. Then she heard the Marquis say:

"Rest for a minute or two. There is no hurry, and you can tell me about it in your own time."

There was something in the calmness of his voice which seemed to give her strength and after a moment she opened her eyes.

"I . . . I am . . . sorry."

"There is nothing to be sorry about," he answered. "Are you all right? Would you like some brandy?"

"No . . . no!" Sona said quickly, "I want . . . nothing. It is . . . just that I . . . ran to . . . find you."

The Marquis sat down on the edge of the sofa facing her and took her hand in his.

Because his fingers were strong, cool and comforting she held on to him almost as if he was a lifeline in a rough sea.

She knew he was waiting, and after a moment she said in a whisper:

"It is . . . there . . . in the centre of the path . . . and it was . . . hidden by . . . twigs and s-sand."

She saw the Marquis's lips tighten and she said frantically:

"It must have been . . . meant for you . . . but I would have . . . stepped on it if it had not . . . been for a . . . rabbit."

She saw the expression in his eyes widen and knew that he suspected she was imagining the whole thing.

"It . . . is true . . . it is true!" she insisted. "You must . . . believe me . . . and I would have been . . . caught in it if I had not been . . . suspicious of the . . . way in which the rabbit . . . behaved."

She was trembling now with the intensity of her words, and also because it had suddenly struck her that if she instead of the Marquis had stepped on the trap she would at this moment be lying drowned in the pool below the cascade. There would have been nobody to save her!

As if he read her thoughts he said very quietly:

"You are safe, and so am I for the moment."

"You . . . must be . . . careful! If . . . somebody is determined to . . . murder you . . . they will now try another . . . way."

"You are sure that somebody wishes to murder me?"

"You . . . said it was your . . . favourite walk."

"It is," he agreed. "I always went there as a boy, and as soon as I returned home two weeks ago it was the first place I visited."

"Then somebody who . . . hates you must have been . . . watching, and planning that was the . . . way they could . . . destroy you."

The Marquis sighed.

"I can hardly believe it. I did not know that my death could be of such importance to anybody living in this vicinity."

"But why . . . else should the . . . trap be . . . there?"

"That is unanswerable," he replied, "and I can only be very grateful that you found it and were clever enough not to be caught in it yourself."

With an effort Sona told him slowly and quietly about the rabbit and how it had seemed so strange that it should turn round for no apparent reason.

"It was then," she said, "that I saw that the surface there on the path had been disturbed, but it was so skilfully . . . covered that probably I would have been . . . looking at the view and would never have noticed it."

She thought of the huge gaping teeth of the trap and shuddered.

The Marquis put his other hand over hers.

"You have to forget it," he said. "You also have to be brave enough to appear at luncheon as if nothing had happened. We would not want anybody else to know about this."

"No . . . of course . . . not," Sona agreed. "That was why I came to . . . find you, and hoped you would be . . . alone."

"It was intelligent of you to think I might be here," the Marquis said. "This is the Estate Office, and as the Agent is busy making arrangements for the Clansmen who will begin to arrive tomorrow, I can work here undisturbed."

"I am so . . . glad I have . . . found . . . you."

"You have a quarter of an hour before you need appear in the Drawing-Room before luncheon. Are you quite sure you can manage it?"

"Quite sure, and you will . . . see about the . . . trap?"

"You are not to think of it any more," the Marquis said. "Leave everything to me, and I promise that neither you, I, nor anybody else will die in that particularly unpleasant manner."

Sona gave a little sigh of relief and as she tried to sit up the Marquis helped her gently to her feet.

He saw how pale her face still was though the stricken look in her eyes was no longer there.

"You can have luncheon in your room if you would prefer it," he said.

She shook her head.

"No, that would worry my father and he would ask questions."

The Marquis was still holding her hand.

"I want to say thank you," he said, "but at the moment it would rather delay things. I will do so later when I can tell you that the trap has been destroyed."

"You will . . . tell me what has . . . happened?"

"I promise I will."

As he spoke he smiled and for the moment he looked very different from the way he had looked before.

The disagreeableness and the scowl had

gone, and instead he was very handsome, very authoritative, and exactly as she thought a Chieftain should look.

Then she remembered that time was passing and as the Marquis opened the door she went through it with just a last shy smile at him and hurried down the passage.

At luncheon the only other people besides herself were the ladies who had obviously spent the morning in bed, her father who had been feeling too tired to go fishing first thing but intended to do so for two hours in the afternoon, and another very old cousin who walked with two sticks.

Sona sat beside her father feeling as if he protected her after all the traumatic terrors of the morning.

"Did you have a nice walk?" he inquired.

"The view from the cairn is very beautiful."

"That is what I used to think. Whenever I came home from school it was always one of the first places I went to."

"I have always thought," one of the London ladies said, "that strenuous walking makes one's legs thick and enlarges the hips."

Sona wished to answer that her legs were very slim as was the rest of her body, then she thought perhaps Lady Jean's thick stocky figure was due to the amount of walking she did.

Then she told herself that was untrue.

Exercise kept one slender and athletic and Lady Jean had inherited her figure from both her parents.

It passed through her mind that it would be a toss-up whether any children she and the Marquis had together would favour their father or their mother, and she found herself thinking how terrible such a marriage must be for him.

Because it upset her she told herself that like the man-trap that was another thing she must not think about.

Nevertheless, she knew it was not only a man-trap that had been set for the Marquis, but a woman-trap also, and she could not save him from the latter.

When luncheon was over Sona still felt shaken and weak so as soon as her father had departed in the pony-trap for the river she went to her own room to lie down.

She tried to read a book, but after a few moments she fell asleep from sheer exhaustion.

When she awoke it was nearly tea-time and Maggie came in to tell her the time and help her into one of her pretty afternoon gowns.

"I were a-wondering, Miss, what ye'll be wearing for th' dancing this eve."

"The dancing?" Sona questioned in surprise.

"Have ye not been told, miss, that His Grace has arranged a performance of Highland Dancing after dinner? And when that is o'er the party'll be dancing reels."

"How exciting!" Sona exclaimed. "I am glad I know how to dance all the different ones."

She was glad her father had been insistent that not only should she have lessons in the dances which were popular in the south, but she should also be proficient in the reels which he said firmly were a part of her heritage.

It had been quite difficult to find a teacher who knew them well enough to satisfy him.

When he did find one, quite a number of her friends had thought it amusing to join in her lessons, and once a week they would solemnly 'Strip the Willow', dance the Eightsome and many other more complicated reels which her father thought she should know.

'I shall not need to be ashamed to take part in the dancing tonight,' she thought, and wondered if the Marquis would partner her in any of them.

The gown she chose to wear was a very pretty one, again in white, but this time it was trimmed with magnolia buds, their dark green leaves a very attractive contrast to the white silk of the gown.

111

In fact, she looked so smart that quite a number of the London ladies looked at her in a way that told her they could not find fault, and she thought there was a glint of admiration in the gentlemen's eyes, however old they might be.

The whole party was very much larger than usual as the Duke had invited a number of neighbours to dinner, and it was a welcome change to talk to people who were not McCarrons but belonged to other Clans.

At dinner Sona sat next to an attractive young man who was a MacDonald and told her stories of his Clan which made her laugh, while her other dinner partner joined in with tales of the Gordons.

In fact, the two gentlemen made the meal a very amusing one, and only as she was laughing spontaneously at something one of them had said did she realise that at the end of the table Lady Jean was sitting sourly without speaking and the Marquis beside her was scowling and looking disagreeable.

"If I were the Marquis I would run away and never come back," Sona thought, but she knew for a McCarron to desert his Clan would be an unforgivable sin.

After dinner they all went into the Chieftain's Room for the dancing that Maggie had told her would take place, and it was very spirited and exciting to watch.

The Clansmen, who seemed incredibly light on their feet, did the sword-dance, and because it was the first time Sona had seen such a performance she applauded enthusiastically.

They danced for about an hour and then the Pipe Band began to play the reels.

Everybody joined in except for the Duke, the relative who walked with sticks and two great aunts, who sat watching.

Sona found that she knew all the steps, and because she was enjoying herself her eyes were shining and her cheeks were pink with the exertion of the dancing.

Her enjoyment seemed infectious and even the more elderly of the McCarrons swung her round while the younger members of other Clans fought to dance with her.

It was getting late and the Duke and several of the elder members of the party had vanished when as a reel finished Sona heard a deep voice beside her ask:

"Will you dance the next one with me?"

She looked up at the Marquis with a smile and replied:

"I would like to do that, but I must first get my breath. That last reel was very energetic."

"So I noticed," he said dryly, "and if you would like some fresh air, come with me."

He did not wait for her answer but walked towards the far corner of the Chieftain's Room and opened a door she had not noticed before.

They passed through it, the Marquis shut it behind them, and Sona found herself in a room which was austerely furnished while the walls were decorated with hundreds of ancient weapons arranged in intricate patterns.

"This is known as the Armoury," the Marquis said as if she had asked the question. "A Chieftain had to have his arms ready so that he could go into battle at a moment's notice."

"I am sure the McCarrons were prepared for anything," Sona replied.

The Marquis did not answer. He was walking to a far corner of the room where he opened another door.

As he did so he picked up one of the large silver candle-sticks which lit the Armoury.

By the light of it Sona could see through the door he had opened a narrow, twisting staircase.

She guessed this was in one of the towers, and as the Marquis went ahead of her she followed him up the stairs holding on to a thick rope attached to the wall which acted as a banister.

When they reached the top he put the candle down on the ground and opened another door.

Now she saw she was on the top of one of the towers that were built at each corner of the Castle.

The Marquis put out his hand to take hers in case she might be afraid of falling over the castellated edge and drew her to where she looked across the sea.

It was a warm night, the stars filled the great arc of the sky and the moon was already high in the Heavens.

It cast a silver light which shimmered over the sea and made everything seem enchanted and quite unreal.

Sona was sure she had stepped into the fairy-tale in which she had always envisaged the Castle standing, and everything that was frightening and unpleasant slipped away.

She was caught up in the beauty of the moon and the stars and the feeling that this was the real Scotland, the land to which she belonged.

For a moment she could not think of anything but the magic of it, not even the man beside her.

Then she heard the Marquis say in a very different voice from the one he had used before:

"Now do you understand why we can none of us ever escape?"

She knew exactly what he was saying and turned to smile up at him and found that he was nearer to her than she had expected.

She could not see his face clearly in the moonlight, but she knew that the fire she had seen last night was there in his eyes, and yet somehow she was not afraid.

She could only look at him and knew that he too was part of the enchantment that was holding her captive, and the reality of anything else had ceased to exist.

Very slowly, as if it was part of the moonlight and the music that seemed to come from the sea, the Marquis put his arms around her.

As if it was inevitable and something that had drawn them to each other for all eternity and was impossible to deny, his lips found hers.

At first he was very gentle and in some strange way his kiss was impersonal.

Then as he felt the softness and innocence of her lips he pulled her closer against him and his mouth became more demanding, more possessive and insistent.

For Sona it was all part of a dream, part of the beauty of what she had felt envelop her ever since she had come north. Part too of her imagination which had made her loyal to the

Clan, even before she had met them, and which was an indivisible part of her heart.

The Marquis drew her closer still and now she could feel the fire on his lips.

It seemed to burn its way through her, lighting a little flame which flickered deep within her body, to rise through her breasts up into her throat, and form the fire that held her lips captive.

She knew then that she had found love, the love she had always wanted, the love that had been an ideal that had always seemed far away on the misty horizon, and so intangible she could not put it into words or even thoughts.

And yet now it was hers and she knew as the Marquis kissed her and went on kissing her that she gave him her heart, her soul so that she could never again be complete without him.

Only when it seemed to Sona that she reached the very zenith of ecstasy and the stars fell from the sky around them and the moonlight enveloped them with a divine light which came too from within themselves did the Marquis raise his head.

With an inarticulate little murmur she hid her face against his neck.

He did not speak, but she felt that he was waiting, and after a moment she said in a voice that was so rapturous it did not sound like her own:

"I . . . love you . . . I love . . . you!"

"I knew the first moment I saw you that you were mine," the Marquis said, "and what I have been looking for all my life."

"How did . . . you know . . . that?"

He smiled.

"How can you ask such a foolish question?"

She knew he meant that they belonged to each other and she whispered:

"I suppose today . . . when I saw that . . . terrible trap that was . . . waiting for you I . . . knew that I loved you . . . but I did not really . . . understand what I felt until this moment."

"And now?" the Marquis inquired.

"I . . . love you so . . . much that I . . . know I am yours . . . completely."

His arms held her so close that it was hard to breathe. Then he said:

"But, my precious, beautiful little Sona, there is nothing we can do about it."

It was then for the first time that Sona remembered he was to be married, and that when the wedding was over she would go back to the south and never see him again.

"How can this have . . . happened to . . . you?" she asked childishly.

"I could not think of any way to prevent it."

"Why did you . . . agree in the . . . first . . . place?"

It was a question she had longed to ask him before, and although somehow it seemed irrelevant at this moment yet because she was close to him, it was something she had to know.

He looked up at the stars and she saw the hard line of his chin before he replied:

"I was tricked by my father in a manner which I am ashamed to tell anybody, least of all you."

"I have to know," Sona said. "It has upset and . . . worried me ever since I came here . . . and I cannot . . . bear to see you . . . suffering."

Her voice broke on the words and the Marquis looked down at her and she could see the lines deeply etched on his face and sense the unhappiness in his eyes.

"I left home five years ago," he said, "because my father would not listen to anything I suggested and refused to move with the times or try to change the conditions of squalor in which many of our people were living. I fought with him and argued with him until the situation was so intolerable that I had to leave."

"You really . . . care about the McCarrons!"

"They are mine, my kith and kin, part of

my blood, from the very lowest to the very highest of them," the Marquis said.

The sincerity in his voice made her very proud, and he went on:

"The situation was so intolerable that I went to London and tried to forget, but all I could do there was to try to influence as many Statesmen as I could, and of course the King, to favour Scotland."

"It is due to you that His Majesty is coming to Edinburgh?"

"It was entirely my idea at the beginning."

"How . . . wonderful of you!"

"We hope great things will come of it, and most of all a new understanding between England and Scotland."

"Go on about . . . yourself."

"I knew from what I was told by members of our Clan, who came to London," the Marquis went on, "that my father was anxious for me to return, not because he wanted my company, but because he was afraid I might find myself a bride in the south."

"And were you . . . doing . . . that?" Sona asked in a very small voice.

The Marquis looked down at her.

"What is true, my sweet, and I want you to believe it, is that I have never in my life wanted to marry anybody until I saw you."

"Is that . . . really true?"

"It is the truth. I have had many love affairs, that you will understand, but no woman has touched my heart or perhaps what you and I would feel was the very spirit of our existence, until our eyes met the first night you dined here."

"I felt something . . . strange pass . . . between us . . . then."

"To me it was not strange," the Marquis said, "but a blinding light which enveloped you like a sign from Heaven. At the same time I knew it was — too late."

Sona gave a little cry of pain, but as if he felt he must tell the rest of the story, the Marquis continued:

"I received a letter from my father saying he was dying and I must return immediately to take his place as Chieftain. I came here with all possible speed, travelling by sea because it was quicker."

"What . . . happened when you . . . arrived?"

"I imagine there was always somebody watching so I should not arrive unexpectedly," the Marquis said, and now there was a cynical note in his voice. "Anyway, as soon as I stepped ashore I was hurried to my father's bedside where I found him surrounded by the older members of the Clan, and with them was the Earl of Borabol."

Sona stiffened. She was already beginning to guess what had happened.

"The light in the room was dim," the Marquis continued, "and there was a minister and a doctor in attendance who told me my father had not long to live."

He hesitated before he said harshly:

"I naturally believed everything that was said to me. Why should I question it?"

"Of course not," Sona murmured.

"I went to my father's side. Weakly he told me that his life had come to an end.

" 'You must take my place at the head of the Clan, Napier,' he said, 'lead them, guide them, and protect them.'

"I will do that, Papa," I answered.

" 'And because it is in the best interests of our people,' my father went on, 'I want you to promise me here, at this moment, that you will join together the McCarrons and the McBoras by your marriage!' "

"What did you . . . answer to . . . that?" Sona questioned.

"I was stunned by the suggestion," the Marquis replied. "For a moment I could hardly believe what my father had said. Then as I hesitated, somebody, I cannot now remember who it was, placed in his frail hands a dirk.

" 'Give me your solemn oath, Napier,' my father pleaded, 'sacred to every Clansman when it is made on the dirk, that you will obey my dying wish. It is the last thing I shall ask of you.' "

There was silence for a moment. Then the Marquis said:

"My father closed his eyes as if the effort had been almost too much for him and he had already died. Then as I knew he still lived and he was waiting just as everybody else in the room was waiting for me to reply, I did as he requested! I swore the oath that can never be broken!"

"It was cruel . . . wicked to ask such a . . . thing," Sona cried.

"I knew I had been tricked when two days later my father rose from his 'death-bed'," the Marquis went on. "He took command of the situation just as he had intended to do and I was forced to travel with the Earl of Borabol to meet his daughter. You have seen what she is like!"

Sona could not answer because tears were running down her cheeks.

She could not bear to think of how hurtful it must have been to the Marquis, and how humiliating to his pride, to realise he had been deceived by some skilful play-acting into swearing away his freedom.

"My darling, I have upset you," he said. "It is something I have no wish to do, but I wanted you to know the truth."

"And now I . . . know it I love you more than . . . ever!" Sona sobbed. "I adore and . . . respect you for doing what you knew was . . . right, even though . . . in fact it was . . . wrong."

"Very, very wrong," he agreed, "because it means I have lost you."

There was so much pain in his voice that Sona forgot her tears and raised her eyes to his.

He looked at her face in the moonlight with the tears glistening iridescent on her cheeks, her eyes swimming with them so that they seemed to reflect the stars in their depths.

"I love you! I worship you!" he said. "You are mine for all eternity! But darling, what is to become of us if we cannot be together?"

For a moment she wanted to cry out at the injustice of it, then Sona realised she could not hurt him more than he had been hurt already.

"I will . . . wait for . . . you," she said very softly. "Perhaps one day God will be . . . merciful to . . . us."

"How can I ask that of you? You are so beautiful, so perfect in every way. You must be married, my darling, to somebody who will look after you and protect you, but I do not think I can bear to talk about it or think of it."

Sona shook her head.

"I belong to . . . you, and I could not let any . . . other man . . . touch me."

"How can you think like that and still be human and real?" the Marquis asked. "You were made for happiness and laughter. If it was in my power, I would give you the stars in the sky and the waves from the sea. But as it is, all I can do is to let you go and leave myself in the darkness of a hell from which only death will release me."

He gazed at her before he said:

"Perhaps it would have been better if you had not saved me from the man-trap."

"No! No!" Sona cried. "You must not think like that! While we are both alive there is . . . hope. I do not know what will happen or how it will happen, but perhaps because I am a little 'fey' I know that one day . . . somehow I shall be with . . . you."

"You mean that?" the Marquis asked.

"I am sure of it."

He drew in his breath.

"I will hope and pray and perhaps after all your name will prove a good omen. You know it means lucky."

"Of course I do," Sona said.

"Sōn-a."

He pronounced it in the Gaelic manner and Sona gave a little cry of delight.

"You can speak Gaelic?"

"Quite well, as it happens. I learnt it as a boy and often later when I was in the south I spoke it whenever I had the chance so that I should not forget it."

"How could I have ever thought you were anything but wonderful, and absolutely right to be the Chieftain of the Clan!"

She knew as she spoke it was only Torquil who had poisoned her mind from the very beginning against the Marquis. Now she felt an overwhelming relief, but she still felt that only because she was clinging to him could she sustain herself.

As if he realised her weakness the Marquis said:

"We must go back, my darling one. I would not have you gossiped about by the busy tongues of our relatives, and somehow tomorrow I will find a chance to talk to you."

He sighed and went on:

"There is so much we have to say to each other, so much that has been bottled up inside me until I feel I am being poisoned by it."

"You must not let it . . . spoil you," Sona said quickly. "Whatever you have to suffer, remember that to me you are . . . everything that is . . . magnificent, and . . . admirable. I

love you . . . I love you, and there are no other
. . . words in which to . . . express it."

Her words brought the fire back into the
Marquis's eyes and once again he was kissing
her wildly, passionately, demandingly. She
felt his need of her was like a raging sea, or a
fiery furnace, and yet she gloried in it.

She knew that his love was as great as hers
and he would never really hurt her.

Only when he kissed her until she felt dizzy
at the sheer wonder of it did he say in a voice
that was raw and unsteady:

"My darling, I must take you back."

He assisted her across the top of the tower,
then went slowly down the twisting staircase
in front of her, guiding her in case she should
slip and fall.

She felt it was symbolic of the protection
he would give her for ever.

She did not know how it was possible, and
yet she knew in some strange and mysterious
manner they were one person and could not
be closer even if they were married.

When they reached the door that led into
the Armoury the Marquis paused.

"I adore you, my darling," he said quickly,
"and as you have told me to do, I will try to
believe that one day the mists will clear."

"I shall be . . . praying they . . . will," Sona
murmured.

Then he opened the door and there was the music of the pipes.

Only when she was alone in her bedroom did Sona feel that everything that had happened was so perfect, so absolutely wonderful, that she possessed a treasure that she could keep in a shrine within herself.

Whatever happened she knew it could never be spoilt, stolen or damaged by human beings or by life itself.

The agony that she must lose the Marquis physically and return south without him would crucify her when the time came, and yet at the same time, because their love came from eternity and would endure to eternity, it would remain unchanged.

Lying alone in her bed she felt his arms were still around her and his lips on hers, and she knew that their love was something which would grow instead of fading, and however far apart they might be, or however much they suffered, that it would remain undiminished.

"I love him! I love him!" she cried into her pillow and thrilled again and again as she repeated to herself the words he had said to her.

It was then she heard the sound of the drum.

It was not near but was distinct, and now

there was no mistaking it as a part of her dreams.

There was a drum playing in the darkness and she thought there was something ghostly about it.

She sat up in bed and with a sudden agony that pierced her like the sharp point of a dirk she thought perhaps the drum was being played not for the Duke, as might be expected, but for the Marquis.

She had saved him from death today, but what about tomorrow and the day after, and the day after that, when she would not be here and anything might happen?

She clasped her hands together listening to the drum which was now fading into the distance.

She had the terrifying feeling that it was a warning specially for her, and tomorrow the Marquis might walk into another man-trap or have a 'regrettable accident' which no-one could explain, except that he would be dead.

"Oh, God, save him!" she cried aloud.

Then in her terror she was praying, praying desperately, jumbling, incoherent prayers that those who hated him would not be successful.

5

When Sona awoke she felt, despite the knowledge that she and the Marquis had to part, that because of their love, the world was golden and the sun was shining more brightly than it ever had before.

It seemed to transform everything that she did, and while the agony of parting was still in the future, all she could think of was that she belonged to him and nothing and nobody could change that.

While she was dressing the Housekeeper came into the room to see if there was anything she wanted, and Sona said to her:

"It is a lovely day and I am so happy to be here."

"That's what we wants ye to think, miss," the woman replied, "an' in the past the Castle were a happy place in which to be."

She insinuated that things had changed, and because she was thinking of the Marquis, Sona said, almost as if she spoke to herself:

"That is what the Marquis must have found when he was a boy."

"He did indeed, miss," the Housekeeper agreed with a warmth in her voice, "an' we used to think it'd be impossible to find a young gentleman who were so bonny and who enjoyed every second o' living, so to speak."

She gave a little sigh.

"We all have to grow older an' that's when the trouble starts."

Sona could think of nothing to say. Then as if the Housekeeper was consoling herself she added:

"But in bad days or in good, the Chieftain'll always be the heart of the Clan."

She went from the room as she spoke and Sona found herself repeating her words.

"The heart of the Clan."

That was what the Marquis should mean to his people, and somehow, difficult though it might be, she must try to inspire him into realising it.

What was more, she must pray that the mists of darkness which covered them both now would one day pass away.

She sent up a fervent prayer that this would happen and felt as if her mother was helping her, and that past members of the Clan were watching over and protecting those who carried on the McCarron traditions.

When she went down to breakfast it was to find only the usual early risers, and she was sure the Marquis had already breakfasted.

Sona ate quickly, determined if possible not to see Lady Jean, feeling her very appearance would upset her.

She had already decided that if she went for a walk alone as she had done the day before she might encounter Torquil, and it would therefore be better to stay with her father and do whatever he intended to do.

This, she discovered as he came to breakfast just before she had finished, was to drive to the river with the other fishers and perhaps throw an occasional line, but otherwise watch them.

"May I come with you today, Papa?" she asked, and knew he was pleased at the idea.

"I shall not be able to fish for long tomorrow when the Clansmen arrive," he said. "I want to introduce you to some of those I knew in the past, and if they are now dead there will be their sons and grandsons to carry on."

Sona knew this would give her father great pleasure. At the same time the fact that the Clansmen were arriving meant there would be only two days left now before the Marquis was married.

She had learnt from her father that they

would camp in the park and on the moors around the Castle.

At night they would light small fires to keep them warm, and it would be difficult to sleep for the noise of the pipes with which they would vie with each other in showing off their skill.

The thought of the music made her remember once again the ghostly drum she had heard two nights running, and she told herself she would always be around in case it pointed to the Marquis.

'I must tell him about it, and beg him to be careful,' she thought.

Then she decided she should protect him from being unduly depressed rather than make things worse than they already were.

Although the Marquis was so authoritative, so commanding, that she felt he took complete possession of her, her love still made her feel protective towards him.

She wished to save him from any suffering either spiritual or physical, almost as if he was her child.

'Love is like that,' she thought with sudden perception and knew, however masterful a man might be, he still needed a woman's tenderness in his life.

Sona and the Colonel set off from the Castle towards the river. The fishers travelled in a brake drawn by two horses, while they drove the small cart drawn by one of the sturdy little ponies which were used out stalking and could climb the steepest moors all day without getting tired.

While they were driving the Colonel talked of the countryside, showing Sona the remains of a fort which had been erected not only to fight the enemies of the Clan, but also as a watch-tower to sound the alarm when the Vikings were seen to be approaching in their long boats.

"It must have been frightening to know that those tall, fair, blue-eyed men were coming from so far across the sea to do battle with them," Sona remarked.

"The Clan often thought that retreat was the better part of velour," her father smiled.

When Sona looked at him enquiringly he explained:

"They had a tunnel which opened not far from the shore and was said to end up on the moors, and although it was meant only for the women and children, I think when the Vikings were sighted the men often used it too."

Sona laughed.

"I call that sensible."

"Of course it was," her father agreed. "The Vikings were twice their size and had superior weapons. After they had done a great deal of damage they would return home with their spoils."

"I would love to see the tunnel."

Her father laughed.

"I have forgotten now where it is. I expect it has fallen in with misuse, but if we have time tomorrow I will take you to a well-preserved fort which is only a mile from the Castle."

"I would like that," Sona said.

She enjoyed seeing three large salmon caught during the morning, and whilst the fishers ate sandwiches by the river, she and her father returned to the Castle for luncheon.

Again there was no sign of the Duke or the Marquis, but the ladies of the party were all there, and Sona sensed that those from London were growing restless and rather bored at the men being away all day, and having nothing to do but talk to each other.

They discussed the Balls they were missing and other festivities that were taking place in the south during their absence.

One of them said to another:

"I am very grateful that His Majesty has not asked us to accompany him to Edinburgh on his visit in August. I wonder if Napier will be in attendance on him."

As she spoke she looked at Lady Jean, and without her saying any more Sona was certain she was thinking that the King, who had always had an eye for a pretty woman, would certainly not wish the Marchioness of Inver to be a member of the Royal party.

It was impossible for Sona not to think how thrilling it would be if she and the Marquis could be in Edinburgh together to watch the excitement of the Scots when the *Royal George* sailed into Leith harbour.

It would be the first time that the King of England had visited Scotland since the reign of Charles II, and when she remembered that the idea had originated with the Marquis she felt very proud that he could do so much for the country to which he belonged.

After luncheon when her father was resting she walked for a little while in the garden, enjoying the flowers that had been skilfully arranged in the beds around the fountain but making no effort to go to the beach in case Torquil should be waiting for her.

The more she thought about his proposal that they should be married by Declaration the more strange she thought it to be, and she was certain there was some ulterior motive besides the fact that he wanted her as his wife.

"He is a very strange young man," she told herself, "and it would be best if I obey the Duke and do not speak to him unless it is impossible to avoid it."

While she did not wish to be rude, he made her feel uncomfortable, and although she was curious she did not like to ask anybody in the Castle questions about him.

The afternoon went slowly, until the fishers came back at tea-time to do full justice to the baps, griddlescones, oat-cakes, and the long loaves of bread filled with currants and sultanas.

They were obviously hungry and boasted about their successes on the river.

"Sometime tomorrow I intend to join you," the Colonel said.

"We will have a sweepstake," one of the McCarrons laughed, "and I shall be annoyed, Mister, if you win, as I have the uncomfortable feeling you might do."

They were all laughing when a servant came to Sona's side saying in a low voice:

"His Lordship asked me to remind you, miss, that you intended to inspect the Armoury at five-thirty."

Sona's heart seemed to turn over in her breast and she said quickly:

"Yes, of course. Tell His Lordship I have not forgotten."

She knew the Marquis had thought of this ingenious method of telling her he would be waiting for her there.

As the ladies drifted away from the tea-table to rest before dinner and the gentlemen retired to the Library where they would doubtless snooze in the comfortable armchairs, Sona sped through the Chieftain's Room towards the Armoury.

When she entered it, it was to find the room empty and for a moment she was afraid she had misunderstood the message and the Marquis meant her to meet him somewhere else.

Then she saw the door of the tower was ajar and she ran towards it.

There was no need for a candle, for the setting sun was coming through the arrow-slits in the walls, and yet after the brightness of the Armoury, it was dim.

Then as she saw the twisting stairs rising upwards the door by which she had entered was shut firmly behind her and she was in the Marquis's arms.

He did not speak, he merely pulled her roughly against him and his mouth took possession of her lips.

He kissed her wildly, passionately, insistently, as if he could no longer control his desire for her and the hours they had been apart had been intolerable.

She felt his burning need of her from the fire in his lips and felt the same flame rise within herself.

He kissed her and kissed her until the fires

of love leapt higher and higher and she felt they were both utterly consumed by it.

Only when her feelings were too ecstatic and rapturous to be borne did she make an inarticulate little murmur and hide her face against him.

"I love you! God, how I love you!" the Marquis said, and his voice was deep and unsteady.

He kissed her hair. Then he asked:

"What have you done to make me feel like this? I had no idea that love could be so overwhelming, so tempestuous. I am like a rudderless ship in a tempest over which I have no control."

"That . . . is what I . . . feel too," Sona replied. "I love . . . you, and there is . . . nothing else in the world but . . . you."

The Marquis kissed her again until they were both breathless. Then he said:

"I did not know a day could be so long or the hours pass so slowly, but I did not dare to see you until now when I knew everybody would be resting."

"That was . . . clever of . . . you."

"We are safe here," he said, "but my precious, we must be very careful. I could not bear that you should be gossiped about or endure the unkind things that could be said if it was known what we felt for each other."

Sona sighed before she answered:

"Yes, and we must be very careful not only in respect of the house party . . . but also that the Clan should have . . . no idea that anything is . . . wrong."

"Why do you say it like that?" the Marquis asked.

He still had his arms around her but his eyes were on her face as if it was impossible for him to look away.

"The Housekeeper said to me this morning that the Chieftain is the . . . heart of the Clan," Sona replied, "and that is what you will be very soon, when they must not only . . . respect and admire you . . . but also . . . love you."

The Marquis pulled her close to him.

"I understand what you are saying to me. But it will be hard, very hard, for me to do what should be done if you are not with me."

"I have . . . thought that . . . too," Sona whispered.

"How can I face the future without you?" the Marquis asked. "I cannot imagine living nearer to Heaven than to be here with you as my wife, to look after our people, to fight for the rights of Scotland, to influence the King to look on us kindly! But I need you, I need you desperately!"

There was a note of pain in his voice which

made Sona press herself even closer to him.

"I am praying," she said, "I am praying all the time that even if I cannot be near you bodily you will know that my mind, my heart and my soul are yours."

"It is not enough," the Marquis answered desperately, "not nearly enough!"

Then he was kissing her again fiercely and passionately until his demands made Sona give a little cry and put up her hands to defend herself.

Instantly his arms relaxed. Then he said:

"Forgive me, my darling. You excite me to madness and I forget how small and fragile you are. I have already sworn that I would never hurt you in any way, but because you are utterly desirable it is difficult for me to control myself."

He kissed her forehead very gently and said:

"I want to lock you up in a tower like this and let nobody see you except me. You are too beautiful for men not to be maddened by your beauty, and I think when you go south I shall go insane with jealousy, apart from anything else."

"There is . . . no need to be . . . jealous," Sona said softly. "There will never be a . . . man in my life but . . . you."

"I am jealous of the air you breathe," the Marquis said fiercely, "jealous of the sun bringing out the gold lights in your hair, and the moonlight which makes your eyes mysterious."

"When you talk like that all the poetry of Scotland is put into words."

"I could write poetry to you," the Marquis replied, "but I would rather fight for you against our enemies, my darling, who are not men-at-arms, but far more insidious, far more difficult to combat."

She knew he was thinking of his father's trickery and the Earl of Borabol, who had been prepared to connive in getting an important husband for his ugly daughter.

"Do not . . . think of it at this . . . moment," she pleaded. "Think of . . . us. We are together and away from the world in an enchanted tower with only the ghosts for company."

"Ghosts who understand and will help us," the Marquis said. "Do you believe that?"

"Of course I believe it," Sona said softly, "and perhaps the ghosts by some magic of their own will bring us happiness."

"All I want is you," the Marquis replied.

Then he was kissing her again.

When they felt as if their legs could no longer sustain them they climbed up the stairs and sat on the top step with the door open so that they could feel the softness of the evening breeze coming from the sea.

The sun beginning to sink in a blaze of glory turned Sona's hair to fiery gold.

There was so much they had to say to each other, yet there were silences when they could only look into each other's eyes.

Then irresistibly their lips would meet as if only by touching and feeling could they satisfy their need, one for the other, and express their love.

At last far away in the distance, they heard the chime of a clock and the Marquis said regretfully:

"Dinner will be in half an hour. We must go back, my lovely one, and as it is you will have to hurry if you are to make yourself even more beautiful than you are at this moment."

He smiled before he added:

"Actually that is impossible because every time I see your face it surprises me."

"I want to do that," Sona answered. "Then you will never be bored with me."

"Do you think that is possible?" he asked.

He kissed her, then closing the door of the tower they hurried down the twisting steps for fear of being late for dinner.

Only as they reached the door of the Armoury did Sona realise that the Marquis was leaving her and she saw that the staircase descended to the floor below.

There was no need for explanation. She knew what he intended to do. He kissed her swiftly but possessively. Then as she walked into the empty Armoury she heard the door close behind him.

She hurried into the Chieftain's Room, ran through it and down the passage to where Maggie was waiting in her bedroom.

"I were wondering what could've happened to ye, miss!" she exclaimed.

"I did not know it was so late," Sona replied.

"I'll help ye, miss, an' ye bath be ready."

With Maggie's help Sona, wearing one of her most attractive gowns, reached the Drawing-Room where they were meeting before dinner with three minutes to spare.

Most of the other guests were already there and so was the Duke. Standing behind his chair was the Marquis.

While Sona curtsied to his father, she was afraid to look at him in case the love in her eyes should be obvious.

"What have you been doing today, Sona?" the Duke enquired.

"This morning I watched the fishers, Your Grace."

"Is it a sport you wish to learn?" the Duke enquired.

Sona was just wondering whether it would

please him if she said she would like to try her skill when the door of the Drawing-Room opened and the Countess of Borabol came hurrying in.

"Your Grace," she said in an agitated manner to the Duke, "I cannot think what has occurred, but Jean has not yet returned to the Castle."

"Not returned?" the Duke enquired. "Where did she go?"

"She went for a walk after tea," the Countess answered. "She is very fond of walking, but I did not expect her to be long. She is not in her bedroom, and the maid tells me she has not changed for dinner."

As the Countess finished speaking the Earl appeared.

"The servants tell me there is no sign of Jean in the Castle," he said to his wife.

The Countess gave a cry which was almost a scream.

"Then what can have happened to her? She must have met with an accident."

"I am sure that is unlikely," the Duke said quietly. "Have you any idea in which direction she went?"

The conversation had now attracted the attention of the other guests, and one of the great-aunts said:

"I saw Jean walking through the garden

when I was sitting in the window knitting."

"Then she might have gone down to the shore," the Duke suggested.

"Is it dangerous there?" the Countess asked.

"No, of course not," the Duke replied, "and the sea has been calm all day."

"Then what can have occurred?"

"Perhaps, although it seems unlikely, she has fallen and sprained her ankle," the Earl suggested, "or she may have walked further than she realised."

"Jean is a very punctual girl," the Countess said. "If she has not returned there is some reason for it. You can be certain of that!"

The Duke fumed in his chair to look up at the Marquis standing behind him.

"Napier, send the servants out to look for your *fiancée!*" he ordered. "Some should go to the beach, some along the cliffs, and alert the stalkers."

"I will do that," the Marquis replied.

He went from the Drawing-Room and everybody began to talk at once, the Countess repeating over and over again that she could not imagine what had happened to her daughter.

They finally went into dinner.

It was an uncomfortable meal with the Earl and Countess finding it impossible to talk about anything but their missing child, and the rest of the party reminiscing about times when they had been lost in the mist on the moors or had other misadventures from which they had to be rescued.

"What do you think has happened?" Sona asked the McCarron who was sitting next to her.

"If you ask me," he said in a low voice, "Jean Borabol is playing the age-old trick of drawing attention to herself."

"What do you mean by that?" Sona asked.

"Well, her prospective bridegroom has not been over-ardent," he answered cynically, "and perhaps she is thinking that absence makes the heart grow fonder."

Sona knew this was the last thing that would happen, but she was forced to say politely:

"Let us hope you are right and she will walk in quite unscathed."

By the time dinner was over and darkness had begun to fall the Countess was growing frantic.

Reports came from the servants that the search for Lady Jean had been quite unavailing.

"Tell them to continue," the Duke said authoritatively. "She must be somewhere."

"The stalkers, the gillies, the woodmen, in fact every man on the estate has now been instructed to search for her," the Marquis replied. "If necessary they will continue through the night, and I am going with them."

"Quite right," the Duke said. "I am sure if anybody can be successful, it will be you, Napier. After all, Jean is your responsibility."

"I am aware of that."

"Oh, you must find her!" the Countess interposed, holding on to the Marquis as she spoke.

"I assure you I will do my best," he promised, "and do not allow yourself to be distressed. I am sure there is a perfectly simple explanation for your daughter's absence."

"I hope you are right," the Earl said, "and I am coming with you. Just wait a moment while I change my shoes."

"Yes, of course!" the Marquis conceded.

When the Earl had hurried from the room there was silence amongst the guests, as everybody was wondering what they should say next.

Then a servant came to the Duke's side and spoke to him in a quiet voice.

"What is this? What man? What does he want?" the Duke enquired.

The sharp way he spoke made everybody in the room attentive.

The servant murmured something again, and the Duke exclaimed:

"If there is somebody who has something to tell us, bring him in. What are you waiting for?"

The Countess moved to the Duke's side.

"The man has news of Jean?"

"I believe so," the Duke replied.

"Then bring him in quickly and let us know what has happened," the Countess begged.

The servant appeared again in the doorway and behind him were two men. To Sona's astonishment one of them was Torquil.

He was looking exceedingly handsome with a well-fitting tweed coat over his kilt, his plaid thrown over one shoulder.

For a moment the Duke was looking at the other man and did not see him. Then there was a frown on his forehead as he asked sharply:

"What do you want here?"

Torquil bowed his head, but it was a proud gesture.

"Angus McCarron, Your Grace, has some information which I thought was of importance for you to hear. As he was too afraid to come alone, I agreed to accompany him."

"Pushing yourself forward as usual," the Duke remarked sarcastically.

"If the man has news of Jean, then let us hear it," the Countess said as if she could not bear the suspense.

Torquil turned to the man beside him.

He was a scruffy, shifty-looking individual, Sona thought, and was somewhat agitated, twisting his cap in his hands and obviously overcome by the Duke and the surroundings in which he found himself.

"Well, what is it, my man?" the Duke asked. "Speak up!"

Angus McCarron, however, was clearly unable to express himself, and after a moment Torquil said:

"Perhaps I should explain for him, Your Grace. Angus has just come to me with a tale that earlier this evening he saw two people walking on the cliffs — a man and a woman."

"Who were they?" the Duke enquired.

"Angus recognised Lady Jean whom he had seen before and he knew she was to be the bride of the Marquis."

"What were they doing? Where was she going?" the Countess questioned.

The Duke raised his hand.

"Wait a moment," he said. "Let us hear the whole story before we ask questions."

The Countess pressed her lips together, and it was obviously very difficult for her to obey the Duke's command.

"These people, you say, were walking along the top of the cliffs?" he prompted.

"That is where Angus saw them, Your

Grace," Torquil replied, "and he thought in fact they were walking very near to the edge. The tide was coming in, and sometimes the spray from the breaking waves can dampen those who encroach too near."

"Yes, yes," the Duke said impatiently. "What happened?"

"Angus says, Your Grace, that he suddenly saw the two people struggling. Then as he watched the man appeared to throw Lady Jean over the edge of the cliff into the sea below!"

For a moment as Torquil finished speaking there was a deathly silence. Then the Countess gave a shrill scream which echoed around the room.

"My daughter! My daughter!" she cried. "She has been murdered! Murdered!"

She threw up her arms as if she was about to collapse and two of the ladies nearest to her hurried to hold her up.

The Duke, however, paid no attention.

"You are saying," he said slowly, "that this man, Angus McCarron, definitely saw Her Ladyship thrown over the edge of the cliff into the sea?"

"That is what he says he saw, Your Grace," Torquil replied.

"I suppose he can speak for himself?"

The Duke fixed his eyes on the Clansman.

"Is this true?" he asked. "And speak the truth, man, or I swear it will be the worse for you!"

"Aye — Your Grace — it be — true!" Angus McCarron answered somewhat incoherently.

"Then tell me," the Duke said, and his voice rose imperiously above the sobbing of the Countess, "if you have any idea who the man might be who accompanied Lady Jean and who you say assaulted her in this criminal manner."

There was no answer until Torquil said:

"Angus McCarron has mentioned a name to me, Your Grace, but he is afraid to repeat it."

"Afraid? Why should he be afraid?" the Duke asked. "However, I presume, as he cannot tell us himself, you are perfectly prepared to do it for him."

Again there was that cynical, almost sneering sarcasm in the way the Duke spoke to Torquil.

Quite undeterred he held his head high and faced the Duke defiantly.

"I will tell you the man's name, if Your Grace commands me to do so," he answered.

"Tell me!" the Duke ordered.

"The man Angus McCarron saw throwing Lady Jean over the cliff was in his opinion undoubtedly the Marquis of Inver!"

Later, when she was in her bedroom, Sona tried to think what she should do.

It seemed like a nightmare when Torquil had accused the Marquis of murder, and yet she was aware in some strange way that everything had seemed to lead up to that moment almost with the smoothness of a theatrical performance which had been skilfully written to extract the utmost drama out of every word.

When Torquil had pronounced the Marquis's name, there was an audible gasp from everybody in the room and several seconds of pained silence before the Duke said, again speaking to Angus McCarron:

"You are sure of this?"

Obviously too frightened to speak, the man merely nodded his head.

"I deeply regret, Your Grace," Torquil said, "to be the bearer of bad news, but I felt it only right that justice should be done, and that you should know what this man has seen."

"What he *says* he has seen," the Duke corrected. "Whether it is true or not will, as you well know, have to be proved."

"I assure Your Grace I appreciate the seriousness of the accusation, but I felt nothing was to be gained by trying to hush-up such an assertion."

"I have no intention of hushing anything up," the Duke said firmly, as if he was speaking to the assembled guests, and not just to Torquil.

"What about — my child?" the Countess cried.

"This man will point out where he thought he saw the crime being enacted," the Duke replied. "Servants will go with him, carrying lanterns and rope."

The Duke turned to the Marquis.

"But you will not go with them. Is that understood?"

"Yes, father," the Marquis replied.

"The Earl, however, should accompany them," the Duke said as if as an afterthought. "Go and tell him what has occurred."

The Marquis did not reply but left the room, and the Duke said to Torquil:

"You are well aware that the mere fact that the information you have just given me comes from you makes me highly suspicious that it is an invention of your overfertile brain, and you are in some way attempting to deceive me, as you have done before."

"I have never done that, Your Grace!" Torquil objected, "although it may please you to think so."

"That is a matter of opinion," the Duke replied.

"You may accompany the search party, and tomorrow, when I have sent for the Sheriff to investigate your accusations, you will make yourself available for questioning."

"Naturally, Your Grace," Torquil replied.

"You can go!" the Duke said, and it was a dismissal rather than permission to withdraw.

Seemingly quite unmoved by the Duke's attitude, and moving proudly with a grace that was undeniable, Torquil turned and left the room, and as he did so he looked deliberately at Sona and the expression in his eyes made her feel embarrassed.

It was as if he told her of his love. At the same time there was also a look of triumph — or was it defiance? — that she could not understand.

Then he was gone, and she felt the nightmare closing in on her.

The Marquis was in danger, and she knew she had the power to save him, but at the expense of her reputation.

She had only to say that at the time when Lady Jean was supposedly walking over the cliffs she herself had been with the Marquis, and he would be exonerated from any suspicion of the crime.

And yet to admit that they had been together for nearly two hours would be to declare openly that they were interested in each other, and that he, an affianced man who was to be married in two days time, had been making love to another and far prettier woman than his future bride.

She wanted, whatever the consequences, to declare immediately that the vile accusations that Torquil had cast on the Marquis through the medium of the frightened Angus were untrue.

As the Marquis finished speaking, she had looked at him, asking his permission to speak.

He had only given her one fleeting glance, then looked away again, but because she was so closely attuned to him she knew he wished her to remain silent, and she therefore said nothing.

But when the search party had left the Castle and everybody was talking in hushed voices about what had occurred, she could not bear to stay in the Drawing-Room any longer.

She slipped away to her bedroom, yet in a way it was worse to sit there wondering what they would find, and if they did discover Lady Jean's battered and drowned body, whether they would be any the wiser as to who had murdered her.

There was always the chance, however,

that she was not dead.

People had fallen over cliffs before now and lived, but if the tide was coming in it would be difficult for somebody who had been dazed by the fall to survive the waves breaking over the rocks and to avoid being carried out to sea by the undercurrents.

"What can have happened? Who can have done such a thing?" Sona asked herself over and over again in the silence of her room, but there was no answer.

She found it difficult to understand Torquil's attitude.

He might hate the Marquis, which had been obvious from the very first time she spoke to him, but being a McCarron himself why should he wish to discredit him in such a manner, and why did it give him so much personal satisfaction?

She had not missed the defiance in his attitude or the way his voice had rung out when he had uttered the Marquis's name.

"He wants to see Napier hanged!" Sona told herself.

But she knew that while she was frightened of the consequence, and whatever she might have to suffer personally by announcing that they had been together, it was not of any importance beside his safety and his position in the Clan.

If there was any doubt as to whether he was the murderer or not, those who came from London would have a juicy bit of scandal to repeat and snigger over when they returned to their own environment.

"What am I to do? What am I to do?" Sona asked herself.

Once again the only answer seemed to be that she must pray; pray for help and guidance, and most of all that the Marquis might be rescued not only from being accused of a crime he could not have committed, but from the scandal and gossip which would be aroused if their love for each other was revealed.

"I must save him! Please God, show me the way!" Sona cried into the darkness.

It was something she went on saying over and over again, and her thoughts became more tortuous, more complicated hour by hour.

"How can this have happened to us?" she asked, as men and women have asked since the beginning of time when something desperate happens and there is the likelihood of the pinnacle on which they have built their lives being destroyed.

'Perhaps,' she thought finally, 'we are being punished because we love each other, and it was wrong for us to do so, as the Marquis is engaged to another woman.'

Yet she knew their love was too great and too perfect for it to be denied. It was something greater than themselves, something greater even than all the conventions by which they were surrounded.

It was overwhelming, omnipotent, eternal and, whatever else happened, the glory of it would remain untarnished within themselves, if not in the world outside.

"Oh, God, I love him so desperately!" Sona cried into her pillow.

At that moment she heard a strange sound at the window.

6

Sona thought she must be imagining it, then the curtains moved and in the light from the moon she saw there was a man climbing into her room.

Her heart gave a frightened leap but she was too afraid to scream. Then with an indescribable rapture she knew who her intruder was.

He pulled back the curtains and now she could see the Marquis quite clearly and she gasped for a very different reason.

"How . . . could you . . . do such a . . . thing?" she asked incoherently, knowing that to climb up the wall of the Castle might have resulted in his falling to his death.

"I had to see you," he said quietly.

He reached the side of the bed and lit the candle which stood beside it.

By the light he could see Sona with her hair falling over her shoulders, her eyes wide with astonishment, but at the same time also soft with the love which she could not conceal.

Their eyes met and she said without thinking:

"I was . . . praying for you."

"I thought you might be doing that."

The Marquis sat down on the side of the bed and put out his hands palms upward, and she laid hers in them.

As his fingers closed she felt a thrill at his touch and he was aware of it.

"I love you!" he said. "I love you so overwhelmingly, that it is difficult to think of anything else. But I have to talk to you, my darling, and this was the only way I could do so."

"It was . . . terribly dangerous and . . . something you must never do again . . . I could not . . . bear it if you hurt . . . yourself."

He did not answer but his lips twisted for a moment, and she knew he was thinking he might be hurt in a very different way if a charge of murder was brought against him.

They were so closely attuned to each other that she could read his mind and she said almost as if he had spoken aloud:

"I must tell the Sheriff . . . where you . . . were."

"Only as a last resort," he said. "Not until I am actually on the steps of the gallows."

She gave a little cry and he went on:

"But I am sure it will not come to that. You

161

and I know that the charge that has been brought against me is a lie."

"I want the whole world to know it," Sona said fiercely.

His fingers tightened on hers.

"All that matters is that you know it," he said, "and therefore, my precious one, you must be patient and say nothing which might hurt you. That I could not endure!"

"But people should not even think such . . . things of . . . you. It is wrong and . . . wicked, and the Clansmen . . . trust you."

"I wonder," the Marquis said as if he spoke to himself. "Because I have been away for so long, I feel they have either forgotten me or think I am no longer concerned with their problems."

Sona was silent. She was thinking of the things that Torquil had said about him.

The Marquis's eyes were on her face and after a moment he said:

"I did not think it was possible for anybody in the world to be as beautiful as you, but I have not come here to make love to you, my precious, and you must help me to behave decently as a gentleman should."

She gave him a little smile and he went on:

"I came to tell you that on no account must we let anybody know what we feel for each other, or reveal that we were together during the time I was supposed to have been committing murder. What is more, it would be easy for people to suspect you were merely trying to save me."

"You mean that they would . . . think I was . . . lying in order to help you?"

He nodded.

She was aware that it would be not unreasonable for the Sheriff and other people to think she had fallen in love with the Marquis, and that she had therefore perjured herself on his behalf.

Then she gave a little cry.

"We have a witness!"

"Who?" the Marquis enquired.

"Maggie, my maid. She was worried because I was so late coming to my room to change for dinner, and only by hurrying did she get me ready on time."

"That is certainly a point in my favour," the Marquis agreed. "At the same time, I have no wish to involve you in this extremely unsavoury affair."

"What do you think really happened to Lady Jean?"

"I have not the slightest idea."

"You do not think one of the McCarrons . . . ?" Sona began.

"Feuds in Scotland linger on for generation

after generation," the Marquis interrupted, "but I think our Clansmen would be too frightened of my father to kill a McBora on our own land, especially one who was to marry me!"

Then after he had spoken he added:

"At the same time one can only guess at what has occurred and just hope her body will be found."

"That would still not . . . explain who . . . threw her over the . . . cliff," Sona said helplessly.

"I know," the Marquis answered.

"Could they really . . . convict you on such . . . flimsy evidence?" she asked in a frightened voice.

"I have a feeling that if those who invented the lie in the first place think it necessary, other witnesses will come forward."

Sona gave a cry of horror and the Marquis said reassuringly:

"I will not have you frightened, and therefore we will not talk about it any more."

He saw she was going to say something and added:

"That is an order, my precious one. Forget it, and think only of our love because it makes you even more beautiful than you already are."

"How can I . . . bear you to be surrounded by . . . suspicion . . . being defamed and . . . insulted?" Sona asked.

"I am sure an explanation will soon be found," the Marquis said optimistically, "but whatever happens, you are to remain silent."

He spoke in an authoritative manner. At the same time he knew he had not convinced her and after a moment he said:

"Please, my adorable one, allow me to know best and do not do anything which might prejudice our future."

She knew as he spoke that he was thinking that if Lady Jean was dead, there was now a hope that they might be together, and it would be sad if slander and suspicion should spoil their happiness.

Sona looked into his eyes and after a moment when she felt he was compelling her to obey him she said:

"You know I will . . . do what you . . . ask me, but it will be . . . hard . . . very hard."

"Thank you, my darling," the Marquis said simply.

He lifted first one of her hands then the other to his lips and now when she felt his mouth on her skin she wanted him to kiss her and moved a little forward, her eyes raised to his.

He looked at her for a moment. Then he said:

"I want more than my hope of Heaven to kiss you and hold you close to me. But, my sweet, because I am here in your bedroom, and because we both know it would be wrong, I dare not touch you."

"I do not believe . . . anything that . . . concerns our love is . . . wrong," Sona said in a low voice.

"Only you could think like that," the Marquis answered. "At the same time we both know what would be said if anybody knew I was here, and because I worship your purity and innocence I will not have it sullied."

He kissed her hand again, then rose looking, she thought, so handsome and attractive that it was only with the greatest effort that she refrained from holding out her arms and begging him to kiss her.

She wanted him so overwhelmingly, so intensely, that she felt as if the fire he kindled in her when he kissed her in the tower was burning its way through her body, and she knew as she could see it smouldering in his eyes that he was feeling it too.

He stood looking at her, and it was difficult for either of them to breathe. Then he said:

"I vow to serve you, to love you and to worship you for the rest of my life."

He spoke very softly, and yet she felt as if it was a proclamation that went forth over the whole land.

"And I will love you with my heart and soul for ever!" she whispered.

The Marquis drew in his breath. Then he bent forward and blew out the candle by the bed and walked across the room towards the window.

"Be careful! For God's sake, darling, be careful!" Sona cried.

He turned his head to smile at her and as he did so he was silhouetted against the moon-light.

Then without speaking he climbed onto the window ledge and she put her hands together in the age-old gesture of prayer.

She prayed and she listened.

After the first moments there was no sound from outside the window and she went on praying until she was sure in her heart that he had reached safety.

She wanted to spring out of bed and make sure that he was not lying spread-eagled on the terrace below, but she told herself to do so would deny her faith in him.

He had come to her in safety, and although it must have been a very difficult climb, she was sure that he would have got down again without incurring an accident.

He had come because he loved her and wanted to protect her, and because his thoughts and his consideration were for her rather than himself.

"He is so wonderful!" she said aloud and

lay with her cheek on her hands where his lips had lingered.

Sona must have slept for a short while and when she woke the darkness in the room had lightened a little and she thought the dawn would soon break.

It was then an idea came to her; an idea so simple that she wondered why she had not thought of it before.

The only difficulty was how she could carry it out.

It was Torquil who had brought Angus McCarron to accuse the Marquis of murdering Lady Jean, and Torquil was the man who had asked her to marry him.

Sona sat up in bed. Then as if activated by the idea that had come to her, she felt, like a ray of light in the darkness, she got up and began to dress.

She would find Torquil somewhere, somehow, and she would tell him that Angus McCarron was lying. Then perhaps he would be able to find the real murderer, the man who had thrown Lady Jean over the cliff.

While she was dressing, she thought it over. She could understand that if Angus had seen two people struggling and thought that the man with Lady Jean was the Marquis, Torquil had been only too eager to accept the

168

supposition because of his own feelings where the Marquis was concerned.

He had made it very clear that he disliked and even hated him, but Sona was sure that Torquil was no murderer.

Yet he would be glad to lay the blame for what had occurred on the Chieftain's son of whom he was jealous, and who had been away long enough to arouse resentment not only in him but also in a number of other members of the Clan.

He did not understand the real reason for the Marquis's absence any more than she had known it until he told her. But now she was certain she could persuade Torquil that he was accusing the wrong person.

As she finished dressing Sona was wondering whether she should go up on the moors and hope that Torquil would find her as he had done before, or to the woods where he had appeared when she had walked through the ride.

Then with a leap of her heart she knew the answer.

The first day she was at the Castle she had seen Torquil rowing his boat and he had said he had been checking his lobster-pots.

She was sure this was something he would do every day, and the pots would be lifted early each morning.

"That is where I will find him!" she thought triumphantly.

She put on the first gown that came to her hand when she opened the wardrobe. When she actually had it on and had tied the sash around her waist, she realized that it was made of thin white muslin.

It struck her that it might be chilly so early in the morning, so she picked up a silk shawl and hurried from her bedroom.

Dawn had by now broken and she thought it must be nearly five o'clock and the servants would be starting work in the Castle.

She had no wish to draw attention to herself and she therefore slipped down the secondary staircase she had used before, but at the foot of it, instead of taking the passage past the Estate Office which led to the front of the Castle, she went in the opposite direction.

She found, as she expected, that there was a door which led out on to the terrace which overlooked the garden.

She saw that the key was in the lock and there were two bolts. She pulled them back easily and was soon running down the long flight of stone steps.

It was too early for the fountain to be playing, for the gardeners had of course not yet arrived to turn it on.

The bees were busy amongst the flowers

and with the first rays of the sun a few butter-
flies were fluttering over them.

She hurried along the gravel path and let
herself out through the gate which led to the
shore.

As she did so she looked back and saw the
curtains were drawn in every window on that
side of the Castle with the exception of her
own.

She thought it was most unlikely that anybody had seen her, in which case she would
not have to answer awkward questions as to
why she had risen so early.

They would think it morbid curiosity on
her part if it was suspected that she was
searching for the body of Lady Jean.

She had no intention, however, of going
further than over the rough ground to the
beach which bordered the bay directly below
the Castle.

When she reached it she looked out over
the sea but found it was impossible to see very
far for the simple reason that there was a
morning mist not yet dispersed by the sun.

She was aware that if Torquil was rowing as
he had before to the jetty she would not be
able to see him until he was very close to it.

She therefore walked to the jetty and sat
down on the edge of wooden slats looking and
waiting, and also saying a little prayer that he

would come this morning as he had the other day.

She must have waited for nearly fifteen minutes and was beginning to feel desperately that she had failed in her quest and would have to look elsewhere.

Then as the mist lightened a little she saw coming towards her the faint outline of a boat.

For a moment it was so indistinct that she could not be sure of it. Then with a leap of her heart she realised it was in fact a boat, and that the man rowing it was unmistakably Torquil.

Because he had his back to her he was not aware that she was there until the boat had actually reached the jetty.

Then as he shipped his oars Sona jumped to her feet and ran to where he would tie up his boat.

"Good morning, Torquil!" she said, and he started.

As he stared at her in surprise she added:

"I am sorry if I startled you, but I was waiting to see you."

"I have been looking at my lobster-pots," he said automatically.

"That is what I thought you would do."

She looked down into the boat and saw there were two large lobsters in the bow, their huge claws groping as if they struggled to escape.

Torquil climbed from his boat on to the jetty.

"You wanted to see me?" he asked.

"I want to talk to you," Sona said.

She felt a little shy as she spoke in case he should think that what she had to say concerned his proposal of marriage.

She did not look at him, although she was aware that he was as usual very smart in his kilt and looked exceedingly handsome.

"I am honoured," he said after a moment. "Where shall we talk?"

Because she was afraid they might be seen, Sona glanced back at the Castle, which was half hidden by the trees which bordered the garden wall.

As if he understood Torquil said:

"If we sit under the wall nobody is likely to see us and be curious."

She could hear the sarcasm in his voice which made her afraid he might begin to be resentful again about his own reception from those who lived in the Castle, and she said quickly:

"What I have to . . . say is of great . . . importance."

"You know I am willing to listen to anything you have to tell me."

Now there was a different note in his voice and she thought he was looking at her face yearningly.

They walked the short distance from the jetty, then crossed the grass towards the high wall.

It was made of the same large grey stones of which the Castle had been built which were rough-hewn and of varying size, which as Sona knew made it possible for a man to climb them.

She forced herself to concentrate on what she had to say to Torquil and found a raised piece of ground covered in grass on which it was comfortable to sit.

"Now explain what is worrying you," Torquil said.

Sona drew in her breath.

"I want to tell you that what you have been . . . told about the Marquis is . . . untrue."

There was silence for a moment. Then Torquil asked:

"You mean about his murdering Lady Jean?"

Sona nodded.

"Whatever happened to her, and whoever she was with, it was not the Marquis!"

"How can you be so positive?"

"Because the Marquis was with me!"

There was silence and for the first time

Sona wondered if she had been unwise to tell him this when the Marquis had told her she must not reveal it to anybody.

But it was Torquil who had brought the man who had laid the charge against the Marquis and, if she convinced him, then the story they told to the Sheriff might be a very different one.

"So he was with you!" Torquil said slowly.

"Yes, we were . . . talking together."

There was another silence. Then Torquil said harshly:

"What you mean is that he was making love to you!"

Sona stiffened.

"There is no reason for you to jump to conclusions!" she replied. "I can swear to you we were together, so it was therefore impossible for him to be with me in the Castle and at the same time on the cliffs with Lady Jean."

She did not look at Torquil as she spoke, but she knew his eyes were on her face.

"Who else knows this?" he asked after a moment.

"Nobody in the house party. They were all resting. But my maid was waiting for me and could therefore testify if necessary that I was late coming to my bedroom to change for dinner."

"So you think this information will let the

noble Marquis off the hook."

She thought his voice was spiteful and she said quickly:

"I know you do not like him, but I am sure that you are honourable and would not like a man to be accused of a crime he had not committed. The Marquis is also a McCarron."

Torquil did not reply, and she went on:

"You have told me that you love the McCarrons, so you must be aware that a scandal like this, whether it is true or untrue, would damage us all. Please, Torquil, speak to that man. Tell him he was mistaken."

"Now you are pleading with me," Torquil said. "This is very different from your attitude when we were last together!"

"If I hurt you then," Sona said quietly, "I did not mean to do so. I was honoured and very touched that you should ask me to . . . marry you, but you took me by . . . surprise, and perhaps I was not as . . . tactful in the way I refused you as I . . . should have . . . been."

"You are certainly being unexpectedly humble at this moment," Torquil remarked.

Sona thought it was something she had no wish to be.

At the same time whatever her own feelings about Torquil, the only thing that mattered at this moment was that she should convince him that the Marquis was innocent and that the charges brought against him must be withdrawn.

"If I am . . . humble it is because I am asking your . . . help about something of the greatest . . . importance to you and to me, and to every McCarron."

"And of course to the Marquis!"

"Naturally! He is the Chieftain's son, and I know you would be the first to realise his importance as the next Chieftain of the Clan."

"The next Chieftain!" Torquil repeated slowly.

Sona put up her hand to lay it on his arm.

"Please, Torquil," she said, "tell that man you brought to the Castle last night he was mistaken, and help us to find the real criminal."

"And are you suggesting that if I do so you will marry me?"

Sona was very still. Then she answered:

"I cannot . . . believe that you would . . . try to . . . blackmail me in such a way."

She forced herself to speak lightly, and to her relief Torquil smiled.

"No, I will not do that, Sona. I have a better idea."

"What is it?"

"I was thinking as I was rowing on the sea just now that I have an idea where Lady Jean might be found."

"You have? You have really?" Sona asked eagerly.

"I am almost certain of it," he said. "Shall we go and look?"

"You mean it is near here?"

"Quite near. You may have heard of the tunnel that was used by our ancestors as a way of escape when the Viking ships appeared."

"I have heard of it!" Sona said excitedly. "But my father said he thought it would have fallen in long ago."

"Some of it is still intact," Torquil said, "and that is where I think Lady Jean's body may be hidden."

"Then we must get somebody to come with us," Sona said. "If she was exploring and got trapped she may still be alive."

"It is certainly an idea," Torquil admitted. "But you will understand I have no wish to make a fool of myself and raise everybody's hopes, only to find there is no sign of her."

Sona could understand that. And the same time she thought it would be difficult to explain, if they fetched other people to help them, why she and Torquil were together.

"I think you are right," she said after a moment. "We should make sure that Lady Jean is there before we ask for help."

"That is sensible," Torquil said. "We had

better go there quickly before the search parties appear."

Sona rose to her feet and followed Torquil who had started to walk northwards along the shore.

As soon as the Castle wall came to an end there was first the wood which bordered the drive, the trees ending high above the shore almost on the edge of the cliffs.

They climbed upwards on some rough steps that had hewn out of the rock.

Then as the trees were left behind the land began to rise covered with thick heather until it became part of the same moor on which the cairn was situated, and also the cascade.

Torquil walked quickly without speaking, and Sona found it quite hard to keep up with him.

At the same time she was excited.

If he was right and they found Lady Jean's body, it would prove that Angus McCarron had been lying when he said he had seen a man throw her over the cliff, and that would be the first step towards the Marquis being exonerated.

They were slowing their pace because the ground was so uneven and the heather, which was old, made the walking difficult.

Then a little to their right Sona could see the round fort which her father had told her was near the Castle, and Torquil stopped.

"The tunnel is here," he said, "and you will understand how it was convenient for those who either lived in the fort or near it."

He walked forward as he spoke and Sona saw there was a clump of gorse bushes in flower and behind them rough ground that did not seem different in any way.

But as Torquil drew her closer she saw behind the bushes there was what appeared to be the entrance to a cave.

The entrance was propped up with one thick pole made of birchwood, and the opening was so small that for the moment Sona was disappointed and felt it would not be the tunnel she had expected.

Then she thought that the sides would have fallen in during the years and as she stared at it, thinking somehow it was unlikely that Lady Jean would be there, Torquil said:

"It is quite safe inside, and there is an exit about fifty yards along."

He pointed as he spoke a little higher up the moor.

"Of course," he went on, "it was much longer in the old days, but you will find what is left is usable and the air is clean."

"And you really . . . think that Lady Jean . . . might be in . . . there?" Sona asked in a low voice.

"The more I think of it, the more I am certain this is where she has to be," Torquil said.

"But how shall we be able to see her?"

"I discovered this passage a long time ago," Torquil replied, "and I have a lantern here somewhere."

He felt among the gorse bushes and brought out a candle-lantern.

He made as if to light it but as he lifted the glass that encircled the candle he exclaimed:

"I think there is somebody coming! Get inside the tunnel! We do not want him to see you."

Hastily because of the urgency of his tone, and also because she thought once again it would be very difficult to explain why she was with Torquil after the Duke had forbidden her to speak to him, Sona obeyed him.

She squeezed herself past the pole which supported the entrance and moved a little way inside.

She could see that the ground was clear as if it had been brushed, and once she was inside it was possible for her to stand upright as the tunnel was both wider and higher that it appeared from the outside.

She straightened herself and looked round. Then she heard Torquil say almost in a whisper:

"Move a little further in. We do not want

him to ask questions."

Quickly Sona took several steps further in, finding she could see her way by the light from the opening.

She thought once again it could be very awkward if anybody knew that she was here.

If the man who was approaching was one of those who were searching for Lady Jean and if he reported her presence to the Duke, what could she say if he asked her why she was with Torquil?

She moved still further into the tunnel, listening for voices outside.

Then suddenly there was a resounding crash.

It seemed to echo along the tunnel and startled her so that she turned round to realise with horror that the entrance to the cave had collapsed and now there was no light at all.

She stood still and for the moment was too frightened in the darkness, to speak.

Then she heard Torquil call:

"Are you all right, Sona?"

"Yes, yes, I am all right," she answered, "but what has happened?"

"I am afraid the entrance has fallen in," he replied, "but do not worry. You can get out at the other end. Just walk along the passage and I will meet you there."

"Is it . . . far?"

Sona felt the tremor in her voice and was ashamed because she was frightened.

"No, not very far," Torquil shouted. "You will be all right. Just walk on and in a few seconds you will see the light."

Slowly Sona turned round again. It was very dark and now alone in the darkness she felt almost as if she was incarcerated in a tomb.

It was so silent that she felt she needed the reassurance that Torquil was there.

"Torquil!" she called.

There was no answer, and her voice seemed to echo back at her. After a moment she called again:

"Torquil!"

She thought he had already moved as he said he would to the end of the tunnel where it came out on the moor.

Then she thought that if she could get out that way, he could come in and guide her with the lantern rather than she should grope in the dark.

'I expect he will think of it,' she thought reassuringly, 'but I suppose I should go on moving.'

She took a step forward. Then suddenly she remembered the trap at the top of the cascade.

She did not know why it was so vivid in her mind, but it was, and remembering how it had upset her at the time, she was afraid now to put her foot anywhere while she could not see where she was going.

She gave an exasperated little sigh.

"I suppose I am being foolish, but Torquil must come and fetch me. After all, he has the lantern."

She put out her hands and found with her arms fully extended she could touch both sides of the tunnel at the same time.

Then she put her hands upwards and as she touched the top she could feel the sharpness of stones and also a little sand or gravel fell on her uncovered head.

"Torquil!" she shouted. "Torquil!"

She thought he should have reached the end of the tunnel by now and would be able to hear her.

But as she listened there was no response.

She felt rather angry that he was not more concerned about her.

Instinctively she took one step forward. Then once again she thought of the man-trap and was afraid.

"Torquil!" she cried again.

Still there was silence, and after a moment as if she was determined to be obstinate she sat down on the floor of the tunnel.

"I will not move until he comes for me," she said. "He must realise it is frightening to be here in the darkness."

Then suddenly, although it seemed absurd that she should not have thought of it before, she remembered why she had come here in the first place — to look for Lady Jean.

If Lady Jean's body had been hidden in the tunnel, then as she stumbled along in the dark she might fall over it.

She felt herself shudder at the horror of finding herself alone with a dead woman, and now she screamed in sudden panic:

"Torquil! Torquil!"

There was only a vague echo and she found herself shivering.

"What can he be doing?" she asked.

She put her hand on the floor of the tunnel and found the ground was firm and moved a foot or so. She did the same again, testing the ground first tentatively with her fingers, then firmly with the palm of her hand before she moved her body forward.

She repeated this several times until suddenly where she felt there was no ground at all but only empty space.

She drew in her breath. Then she moved backwards a little way as still nervously she tested the ground in front of her terrified that her hand might suddenly be caught in the teeth of a man-trap.

As she did so she dislodged a small stone.

She felt it fall, then a second later heard a

soft 'plop' as it landed far below in what she guessed must be water.

It was then she was aware that in front of her was a hole and there was fresh air coming from it.

She felt around her and found another stone and dropped it over the edge.

Now there was no doubt that there was a splash, a very faint one, and yet because she was listening she could hear it.

It was then she realised that if she had done as Torquil told her and walked along the tunnel to where he had said he would be waiting for her, she would have fallen straight down like the stone perhaps to be drowned, as anybody falling over the cascade would have been.

Sona drew in her breath.

It was then at that moment, that she knew clearly and unmistakably that Torquil was the murderer, and that he had not only killed Lady Jean but in doing so had contrived that the Marquis would be hanged for a crime he had not committed.

Sona must have sat still for an hour before she moved slowly back to the entrance to the tunnel to see if that way there was any escape for her.

When she touched the fallen earth with her hands she realised that if, as she now suspected, Torquil had pulled away the wooden support, it had dislodged an enormous amount of earth and stones which it would be impossible for her to clear away by herself.

The blockage was so thick that there was not even a chink of daylight showing through it, and she was afraid to try to move even a little of it in case more descended on her head.

It was a very skilfully constructed trap and she wondered how he had managed to put it into position so quickly after Lady Jean's death, if he had enticed her into it in the same way.

Then she thought he might have used a different method for her and had merely suggested showing her the tunnel. Then when they reached the hole he had pushed her into it before she even realised it was there.

It seemed incredible that Lady Jean should have gone with him so trustingly, and yet Sona would not help admitting wryly that she herself had trusted Torquil completely.

He was so handsome and could exert such charm when he chose, and she was quite certain that if he had met Lady Jean out walking and suggested she might like to see the Viking tunnel, any woman, especially one so unattractive, would have found it difficult to refuse what he asked.

"How can I have been so foolish as to think he would help me?" Sona asked herself.

She knew now that it was because she had said she could provide an alibi for the Marquis that Torquil had decided to kill her.

She went over their conversation, thinking she knew the very moment when he realised that she was dangerous to his plan and he must dispose of her as he had disposed of the Marquis's future wife.

"But why? And how will it benefit him?" she wondered.

She wished she had not been so foolish as not to have made her father tell her about Torquil after he had said he would find out who he was.

'I deserve to be in this predicament,' she thought.

Then she knew that if she died she would never see the Marquis again, and what was more she would not be able to save him from being convicted for the murder of Lady Jean.

"I must save him! I must!" she said aloud.

She was sitting just inside the entrance to the tunnel and she wondered whether, if she screamed loud enough, anybody would hear her, then knew it was unlikely.

She felt sure the search parties of the night before had gone carefully over all this part of the ground.

Yet they might come again, and she told

herself the only sensible thing to do was to listen and if she heard the slightest sound to scream as loudly as she could and hope that somebody would hear her.

It was very eerie just listening and not moving.

Outside the sun would be shining and there would be the buzz of the bees and the sound of the waves and the cry of the gulls, but in the tunnel there was only silence — a silence in which Sona thought she could hear the beat of her heart.

After listening a little while she began to pray for help to God, then to the Marquis.

Because she loved him so desperately she thought he must be aware of the danger she was in, and he would save her as she had saved him from the man-trap that had been set just above the cascade.

"Save me! Save me!" she called first in her mind, then in a whisper that seemed to make the darkness even more ghostly and frightening than it was already.

"Save me! Perhaps God will put in your . . . mind where I am . . . likely to be."

She thought that if they had ever talked of the tunnel together he might think of it, but she had spoken of it only with her father and it was unlikely that he would remember the conversation.

She reckoned that by now they would have had breakfast at the Castle, but nobody would think it strange that she was not there, and it would be very, very much later in the day before anybody would begin to worry as to where she was.

Perhaps by luncheon time someone would ask for her.

Then she remembered that her father had said they would go this morning and meet some of the Clansmen who were to be found camping in the park.

She wondered if any of them would be on this side of the wood, and thought it unlikely.

It would stand as a barrier between them and the Castle with their Chieftain so it was probable that they would all be on the other side of the wood or on the moors above.

Again she sat listening, but no sound came through the fallen earth, and now she began to be really afraid in case she was to remain here until she died, and it would prove a tomb not only for Lady Jean, but also for herself.

"Please God help . . . me . . . please . . . please," she prayed.

It must have been nearly five hours later that suddenly there was a sound that startled Sona.

Strangely enough, she had been half asleep, hypnotised by the darkness and the repetition

190

of her prayers until she began to feel she was drifting away from reality and was no longer herself.

Then the sound came again, and now, although it was very faint, it was unmistakably a voice.

She gave a little cry and realised that it was strangled in her throat.

She tried again.

"Help! Help!"

But then there was only silence and she supposed she must have been mistaken.

Then she realised that if somebody had heard her they would be listening for her to cry again.

"Help! Help!" she called as loud as she could. "I am here. Oh, please . . . help me!"

It was then, almost, she thought, like a voice from Heaven, that somebody shouted:

"Be there anybody there?"

"Help! Help!" she cried and now a voice she knew, a voice that brought her back to life, replied:

"Sona? Is that you, Sona?"

She gave a little cry of happiness, then the tears were running down her cheeks as she answered:

"I am . . . here! I am . . . here! Oh, Napier . . . save . . . me!"

7

Sona sobbed all the way back to the Castle in the Marquis's arms.

When he first got inside the tunnel, having dug away the opening, she thought he was like St Michael coming down from Heaven to save her.

She had been listening to the men working outside with the tears running down her face, and only when finally the Marquis was beside her and she could cling on to him did she realise how cold and frightened she had been.

"It is all right," he said quietly, "you are safe now, and I swear that nothing like this shall happen to you again."

She could hardly understand what he said, but was only conscious that he was there, that she was close to him and the terror she had endured was over.

Nevertheless the shock had now caught up with her, and by the time they reached the Castle she was almost unconscious.

The Marquis carried her up to her room. Then there was a warm drink, hot bottles at her feet and a dozen people to tend to her after he had left her.

Only very much later did she understand it was only by a lucky chance that she had been saved, the luck which was there in her name.

A stalker had got up unusually early to begin his search for Lady Jean as he had been told to do. He had gone high up on the moor and lay down in the heather to look around with his spy-glass.

The mist was over the sea and he was just about to look in another direction when he saw two people walking on top of the cliffs.

He thought it must be the first of the search parties coming from the Castle and he would have taken no notice if one of them had not been a woman dressed in white.

There was no woman in the village who was likely to wear a white gown, and he therefore assumed that the person wearing white was a guest in the Castle.

It was difficult to see clearly, but as he watched the two people with a vague curiosity, he suddenly became almost certain that the man was Torquil.

He knew him well and his amorous adventures with the local girls were the subject of many jokes amongst the Clansmen.

The stalker thought it strange that Torquil should be with a lady from the Castle, and as he could see them quite clearly being by now out of the sea mist, quite suddenly the lady in white disappeared.

The stalker thought he must be mistaken and refocused his glasses.

Then he saw Torquil going quickly back to the jetty and some minutes later he saw him walking along the sands towards the village carrying a lobster in each hand.

He was not a very intelligent man, and it took him a little time to consider it odd that the lady in white had disappeared so completely.

Then he saw other search parties coming from the direction of the Castle.

They were moving along the cliffs and on the beach and as far as he could see there was no woman amongst them.

After he had watched the search parties for some time, it struck him that perhaps he should report the fact that he had seen a woman in white with Torquil.

He was, however, nervous of making a fool of himself unless of course Torquil had been clever enough to discover Lady Jean when everybody had failed the night before.

In which case, why had he not taken her back to the Castle?

Without hurrying the stalker had come down from the moor and gone to the Castle to speak to the Duke's agent.

He met various Clansmen and other stalkers on his way there, but thought it best not to discuss with them what puzzled him.

When he reached the Estate Office, still not quite certain whether or not he should keep what he had seen to himself, he found the Marquis there.

The stalker was an elderly man who had known the Marquis since he was a boy, and they had done many stalks together and brought home their stags in triumph.

"Nice to see you, Andrew," the Marquis said, holding out his hand.

After making polite enquiries about the old man's family, the Marquis said:

"I should have asked you at once why you are here. Have you anything to report?"

"I dunna ken if it be of any reel import, M'Lord . . ." the stalker began.

But what he related to the Marquis made him run from the office to find out if Sona was in the Castle.

It was then he learned that her father was extremely annoyed because he was waiting to take her to meet some of the Clansmen who had been gathering in the park ever since day-light.

When the Marquis told the Colonel what the stalker had told him he exclaimed:

"From what you tell me, Sona and that man must have been near the Viking tunnel. I was talking to her about it yesterday."

The Marquis had not waited for any more but had set off with the stalker at a pace which made it impossible for Colonel McCarron to keep up with them.

As soon as he realised what had happened the Marquis sent Andrew to fetch other men to dig away the fallen entrance to the tunnel.

"How could you have done anything so foolish as to go with that man Torquil to such a place?" Sona's father had asked when she had recovered enough for him to talk to her.

"He said he . . . thought . . . he . . . knew where Lady Jean . . . was," she answered.

There would have been far more commotion about Torquil's attempt to murder Sona after they had found the body of Lady Jean, if something even more sensational had not occurred.

When the Duke learned that Torquil was the murderer and realised the significance of a McBora being killed on McCarron ground, he had fallen into such a furious rage that he had a heart attack and died.

Sona heard the bell tolling which was only rung when a Chieftain died, and at first could

196

not understand the reason for it.

Then her father had come to her room and sat beside her and told her what had happened.

She felt an irresistible feeling of joy that now the Marquis could take his rightful place as Chieftain of the Clan and would no longer be overshadowed by his father and in danger of being tricked by him as he had been before.

But she did not say anything and her father had gone on:

"As soon as the funeral is over we must return to the south. Napier will have a great deal to do and the last thing he will want is a large house party of his relatives."

Sona made a little sound and her father added:

"There is also the question of what is to be done about Torquil."

This was something that she had been wanting to ask, but felt too weak to do so.

"I blame myself," her father said in a low voice, "for not telling you before what he was like, but of course after the Duke had told you not to speak to him I had no idea there was any likelihood of your doing so."

Sona felt guilty, knowing how she had talked with Torquil by the cairn and in the woods, and had deliberately gone in search of him to ask his help.

She was wondering if she should tell her father of this when he continued:

"It is such an unpleasant story that I had no wish for you to listen to it. Now I think you should know why he behaved as he did."

"I want to know that, Papa."

"When I first came to the Castle," her father began, "there was a very pretty housemaid here called Bessie Ross. Everybody liked her, and as she was very efficient she quickly rose to being Housekeeper, although she was really too young for the job."

Sona was listening intently as her father continued:

"It was a great shock therefore to the Duke when Bessie informed him that she was having a baby and the father was one of the guests who had stayed at the Castle."

Sona felt this would account for the fact that Torquil looked like a gentleman.

"Because the Duke felt in some way responsible," her father went on, "he gave Bessie a house in the village and when her son was born had him educated at a school in Edinburgh. She was naturally the object of scorn locally but it did not appear to trouble her, and when Torquil grew older he considered himself, in a way rightly, to be a cut above the boys of his own age who had not had his education."

"So his position made him bitter," Sona murmured.

"I suppose that was inevitable," her father agreed. "Then when Torquil came of age he began to call himself Torquil McCarron instead of using his mother's name of Ross."

"What right had he to do that?"

"None," her father replied, "but he came to the Castle and informed the Duke that he had discovered that his father was in fact a McCarron and the Chieftain's first cousin."

Sona remembered that this was what Torquil had said to her and she asked:

"Was it true?"

"No, of course not!" her father replied. "Bessie had told a very different tale when she first informed the Duke she was pregnant, and there was no question of Torquil's father being a McCarron. But he insisted that not only was Neil McCarron his father, but he was married by Declaration to his mother, and he could produce witnesses to prove it."

Sona remembered that was the sort of marriage Torquil had suggested to her, and now she understood that he wanted to marry her not only because perhaps in his own way he really wanted her as his wife, but also because it would further his ambitions to be a member of the Clan.

She, however, did not interrupt her father who went on:

"The Duke refused to accept such claims, saying that they were completely untrue. At the same time he realised that Torquil could make a great deal of trouble because, if he actually was Neil McCarron's legitimate son, then until Napier produced a child he would be his heir presumptive."

"I cannot believe it!" Sona exclaimed.

"I am afraid that was what was in his twisted mind," her father said, "and of course when the Duke forced Napier to become engaged to Jean McBora it put paid to all Torquil's aspirations."

"So that was . . . why he . . . murdered her!"

"Exactly!" Colonel McCarron agreed. "But I cannot understand why he should wish to murder you also."

It was then that Sona had to tell her father the truth recounting how Torquil had proposed to her, how she had been with the Marquis at the time Angus was supposed to have seen him pushing Lady Jean off the cliff.

Shyly she added that she had thought that since Torquil loved her he would do what she asked and prevent Angus from giving evidence that he had seen the Marquis when it was not true.

She held tightly on to her father's hand as

she confessed the whole sad story, and although she had been afraid he might be angry when she finished he had only said:

"I can only thank God, my dear, that you were saved from dying by a chance that might happen to one person in a million."

"I am . . . sorry to have . . . been so . . . foolish."

"It was very understandable in the circumstances. I will tell Napier what you have told me, but I feel sure there will be no reason for anybody else ever to hear of it."

"And . . . Torquil?"

"When he learnt that you had been found and brought back to the Castle he disappeared."

"How?"

"He was seen rowing across the bay and neither he nor his boat have returned."

"Do you . . . think he . . . will come . . . back?"

Her father shrugged his shoulders.

"I think he will either reach the coast of Aberdeen, although it is a long way, or else if the sea grows rough there is every chance he will be drowned. Either way, I am quite certain we shall never hear of Torquil, by whatever name he calls himself, again."

After her father left her, Sona had slept and when she awoke it was to hear the bagpipes playing laments, and four days later she and her father had sailed for the south.

It was Napier who decided they should travel that way, which would be the most comfortable for her.

Although he was engaged every moment of the day first with the preparations for the funeral, then the ceremony of receiving the homage of the Clan, now he was their Chieftain, she knew without being told that his thoughts were with her as hers were with him.

The female members of the household, as was usual in Scotland, took no part in the funeral itself.

They were only allowed to see the Duke as he lay in state in the Chieftain's Room, covered by his own standard, with four Clansmen guarding him who were relieved by four others every two hours.

Her father insisted that Sona was not well enough even for that ordeal, and as the doctor agreed with him she stayed in her room until the funeral was over.

It was then she learned that Napier had told her father of their love and that they would be married as soon as it was possible.

He, however, insisted that because he must start his new life correctly nobody must suspect their fondness for each other until some months had passed.

"He is thinking of you, my dear," the Colonel explained to his daughter, "and I am doing the same. So we are going back to Derbyshire until it is possible for you to be married, in which case when you come north again so shall I."

Sona looked at him questioningly and he explained with a smile:

"Napier has given me a house not far from here, and for me it will be like coming home."

"Oh, Papa, how wonderful! I know it will make you happy, and even when I am married Napier knows I would want you near me."

"I thought you would feel like that," her father said simply, "and as you say, it will make me very happy."

Because they had to be careful that their relatives should not guess their secret, Sona had only a few minutes alone with the new Duke before her journey south.

It was her father who told her where to find him.

"Before we leave," he said to her, "I think you should see the view from the North Tower. I am sure you can find your way to it by yourself."

He had only to look at the radiance on Sona's face to know that she understood what he was saying.

"We will go together to the Chieftain's Room," Colonel McCarron went on, "and I shall be there if you want me."

Sona knew he was guarding her against the intrusion or suspicions of anybody else in the Castle.

She felt as if she flew on wings rather than walked as she crossed the Armoury, and found that the door to the tower was open.

Then Napier's arms were around her and he was kissing her wildly, passionately, demandingly, in a manner which told her that he was thinking how easily he might have lost her.

Only when they were sitting as they had before on the top step of the stairs to the tower was she able to speak.

"I love you!" she said.

"Your father has told me," Napier said, "how you met that fiend to try and save me. My precious, how could you have taken such a risk?"

"How could I have . . . known that he was the . . . murderer?" Sona asked.

"We will not speak of it again," Napier said, "because it terrifies me to think I might never have found you."

"I was praying that you would."

"I had completely forgotten about the Viking tunnel, and only somebody like Torquil would have realized the possibilities it contained for disposing of anybody in a way that was extremely unlikely to be discovered."

"What was the hole in the middle of it for?" Sona inquired.

"It was how the Clansmen obtained fresh water when they were in hiding from the Vikings. It must originally have been quite a small well, used presumably when necessary by those who were in the Fort, and there is a drop of about twenty feet down to a burn which comes from the hills."

"And that was . . . where Lady Jean was . . . found?" Sona asked in a low voice.

"I think Torquil must have pushed her head first. She was knocked unconscious when her head hit the stones at the bottom," Napier replied. "There is not much water down there, but enough to drown somebody who had fallen face downwards."

Sona drew in her breath at the horror of it and he went on:

"In stormy winter weather the burn would become swollen and then the body might have been washed out to sea."

He paused before he said in a voice she could hardly recognise:

"It might have happened to you, my precious!"

Then he was kissing her again, and because

it was so wonderful to be in his arms and to feel his lips on hers, Sona could remember nothing except that she loved him and that he was arousing a flickering flame which was beginning to burn its way through her body.

Only when she felt they had reached Heaven and touched the divine did Napier say:

"You must go back to your father, my darling. You leave tomorrow and it will be an inexpressible agony to see you go, but it will not be for very long."

"How . . . long?"

It was difficult to speak because she was so excited by the closeness of him and the sensations he had aroused in her.

His heart was beating as violently as hers and there was the unmistakable fire in his eyes that told her how much he wanted her.

"I have been talking about this to your father," he said after a moment.

"What did Papa say?"

"He said perhaps we need not wait the whole twelve months of mourning, as is conventional, and that we can be married at Christmas."

"Oh . . . Napier!"

Sona's eyes were shining like stars. Then because she was a woman she could not help asking:

"You are quite . . . certain you will not have . . . forgotten me by then and no . . . longer want me?"

"It is I who am afraid that you may fall in love with somebody else," he answered. "And if there is any likelihood of that, I swear I will marry you here today, and be damned to what anybody may say about it!"

"That is what I would . . . like to . . . do," Sona whispered, "but it would be . . . wrong for you . . . and you know as well as I do that it would . . . shock the . . . Clan."

The new Duke's lips twisted in the cynical smile that she remembered.

"They are watching me warily," he said, "wondering if all the tales they have heard of my life in the south and the lies spread by Torquil are true."

"I know how . . . wonderful you are and that you are . . . everything they . . . need and . . . want," Sona said. "That is why we must do what is . . . right."

"I believe with your guidance and inspiration I shall be a model Chieftain."

"You will be the heart of the Clan, which is what I want for you," Sona replied.

Then his lips were on hers so that it was impossible to talk, but only to feel.

Carrying a sprig of mistletoe which she

had found in the orchard, Sona walked slowly back to the house.

It was a crisp, frosty day, and the paths were covered with ice so that she walked carefully in case she should slip.

Next week it would be Christmas and every morning when she woke she thought there was only another few days, then perhaps hours before she would see Napier again.

The Social Column in *The Times* had told her that he had come south to be in attendance upon the King, and she had felt her heart leap as she read it.

She was sure that was not the only reason for his leaving the Clan, and there was another and much more personal one.

It had been hard not to feel lonely and left out when she had read of the part he had played during the visit of the Monarch to Edinburgh last August.

The papers had been full of the Reception which the King had received and the delight he had caused when at the Caledonian Ball he had asked for Scottish Reels.

Amongst the gallant Highlanders who had welcomed him had been a new Duke of Invercarron, and Sona had known that however many other Chieftains had been there he would have stood out amongst them.

She had written to him and he had replied

with short letters which told her little except that he loved her.

She could understand that he found it difficult to express himself on paper.

Although she wrote of the things she was doing with her father she had the feeling that for him, like herself, what mattered was the words of love at the end of the letter and the fact that her hands had touched the paper.

He had not said when he would come to Derbyshire, but she knew it would be soon and she was using the time of waiting in collecting together her trousseau, thinking that every gown was important because he would see her in it.

At the back of her mind she was always a little afraid that, because he had been so long in London and known so many beautiful women, he would find her dull and countrified.

And yet she knew this was really only a superficial fear for deep down in her heart she was aware they belonged in a way that made them indivisibly a part of each other for all eternity.

There had been many other things to do besides buying her trousseau, for all her father's and mother's treasures which they had accumulated over the years had to be packed ready to go north.

Now in fact there was left only the room in which they habitually sat and their bedrooms.

It was extraordinary how much would have to be taken with them, pictures, and china, trinkets, books and little things which her mother had loved because they were reminders of moments of happiness, either with her husband or her child.

"I know I am going home when I go north," her father said, "but I still want to take my home with me."

Sona had understood what he was trying to say, and she was determined that she would personally arrange his new house to look very much like the one in which he had lived for so many years and found such happiness with her mother.

She went on hoping that perhaps he would find somebody to share his life with him, but she knew in the meantime it would mean a great deal to him to be amongst his own people, and be able to have all the fishing and shooting he desired.

Because Sona felt so happy she was humming a little tune as she walked from the orchard into the garden.

As she did so, she had a glimpse of the front of the house and saw standing outside the front door a closed carriage drawn by six horses.

Her heart seemed to turn six somersaults, then she started to run, but was hampered by her long, fur-lined cloak which she picked up with both hands so that she could move quickly.

She sped into the house by a side door, then without even pausing to think burst open the door of the Sitting-Room.

He was there, standing in front of the fire, and she stopped still at the sight of him, her eyes shining with joy, seeming to fill the whole of her small face.

It struck her he looked different.

Then she realised it was because she was seeing him for the first time not in a kilt, but in the conventional cut-away coat and the tight-fitting champagne-coloured pantaloons of an English gentleman.

He wore highly polished Hessians and his white cravat was tied in the latest fashion.

It was, however, not his clothes that concerned Sona but the expression in his eyes and the smile on his lips.

Then as they stood looking at each other and the air around them seemed to vibrate with the intensity of their feelings, the Duke opened his arms.

At last the spell which had held Sona still in the doorway broke, and she ran towards him.

He pulled her against him, holding her closer

and closer until his lips came down on hers.

She knew then all her fears that he might have forgotten her and no longer needed her were foolish and quite unnecessary.

He wanted her as she wanted him, and now they were together and nothing and nobody would ever separate them.

"I have . . . missed you!" she whispered.

"And I have missed you, my darling," he said in his deep voice.

He pushed her fur-edged hood back from her head.

"My Christmas bride!" he said, "and I do not intend to wait one moment longer than I have to."

"I feel we have . . . waited already for a million . . . centuries," Sona murmured.

Then he was kissing her and it was impossible to speak. She could only surrender herself completely to the demand of his lips. . . .

A long time later when he had taken off her cloak and she was sitting on the sofa by the fire with her head on his shoulder, he said:

"I have made all our plans. My own chaplain is joining us tomorrow and will marry us in a proper Scottish Service in any Church we can borrow for the occasion."

"Tomorrow!" Sona exclaimed in surprise.

"I must have you alone, my darling, for a

short while before we return to Scotland, for all the festivities there must be for the marriage of a Chieftain."

"That is . . . what I would . . . like."

"And it is what I intend to have," the Duke said firmly, "and to make sure we have a proper honeymoon we have been loaned a house not far from here."

"Where we can be . . . alone?"

"Completely alone. The Viscount Curzon is in London in attendance on the King, and you will find Kedleston a magnificent and fitting background where I can tell you of my love and teach you, my lovely one, to love me."

"I do that . . . already."

"Not as much as I want you to," the Duke answered.

He pulled her closer to him and said:

"I think I am still afraid, desperately afraid, I may lose you at the very last minute, as I so nearly did before."

She knew he was thinking that he might have lost her either because she had been murdered or through his enforced marriage to Lady Jean. Since she could not bear to think of the dangers they had passed through she said quickly:

"Tell me about the Clan."

The Duke smiled as if he understood the question.

"I think without conceit that they are now rather pleased with me as their Chieftain. I have started many improvements that I want to tell you about, new houses, new schools, and I hope it may be possible to introduce new industries which will bring prosperity to the poorer of our people."

"I want to . . . help you."

"I shall insist that you do. In fact, my adorable one, there will be so much for you to do that it will only be very occasionally that we will be able to visit London to show the King, and of course the Social World, how beautiful you are."

"I only want to be certain that *you* think I am beautiful," Sona murmured.

"I shall be telling you that every day and every moment we are together," the Duke said, "and kissing you to make sure that you believe it."

His lips held her captive. When he raised his head he looked down at her, and his fingers ran down the side of her face and along the line of her chin.

"You are the wife I always dreamt about and hoped one day I would find," he said, "but I was afraid I would be disappointed."

"I will try not to . . . disappoint you," Sona murmured.

"You will never do that," he answered. "It

is not only your beauty which draws us together; something which comes from our hearts and what you said was our spirits. It is also the spirit of Scotland."

"That is what I believe," Sona said, "but oh, my darling, wonderful Napier, because it seems like a dream, please marry me very quickly in case I wake up."

The Duke laughed tenderly.

"It is a dream we will dream together," he said, "and we will make our people dream it, too, and so the history of the McCarrons for the next hundred years will be not of warring, but of happiness and love."

"That is what I want you to say, and that is what will make you a great Chieftain," Sona cried.

"That is what with your help I will try to do," the Duke promised.

There was a serious note in his voice which told Sona he meant it with all sincerity.

Then he was kissing her again, and it was impossible to think of Chieftains of Clans or even of Scotland, but only of love which filled their hearts and came from the heart of God Himself.

The employees of Thorndike Press hope you have enjoyed this Large Print book. All our Large Print titles are designed for easy reading, and all our books are made to last. Other Thorndike Press Large Print books are available at your library, through selected bookstores, or directly from the publishers.

For more information about titles, please call:

(800) 257-5157

To share your comments, please write:

Publisher
Thorndike Press
P.O. Box 159
Thorndike, Maine 04986

VAN READER RECORD-A

1	11	21	31	41	51	61	71	81	91	101	111	121	131	141	151	161	171	181	191
2	12	22	32	42	52	62	72	82	92	102	112	122	132	142	152	162	172	182	192
3	13	23	33	43	53	63	73	83	93	103	113	123	133	143	153	163	173	183	193
4	14	24	34	44	54	64	74	84	94	104	114	124	134	144	154	164	174	184	194
5	15	25	35	45	55	65	75	85	95	105	115	125	135	145	155	165	175	185	195
6	16	26	36	46	56	66	76	86	96	106	116	126	136	146	156	166	176	186	196
7	17	27	37	47	57	67	77	87	97	107	117	127	137	147	157	167	177	187	197
8	18	28	38	48	58	68	78	88	98	108	118	128	138	148	158	168	178	188	198
9	19	29	39	49	59	69	79	89	99	109	119	129	139	149	159	169	179	189	199
10	20	30	40	50	60	70	80	90	100	110	120	130	140	150	160	170	180	190	200

VAN READER RECORD-B

1	11	21	31	41	51	61	71	81	91	101	111	121	131	141	151	161	171	181	191
2	12	22	32	42	52	62	72	82	92	102	112	122	132	142	152	162	172	182	192
3	13	23	33	43	53	63	73	83	93	103	113	123	133	143	153	163	173	183	193
4	14	24	34	44	54	64	74	84	94	104	114	124	134	144	154	164	174	184	194
5	15	25	35	45	55	65	75	85	95	105	115	125	135	145	155	165	175	185	195
6	16	26	36	46	56	66	76	86	96	106	116	126	136	146	156	166	176	186	196
7	17	27	37	47	57	67	77	87	97	107	117	127	137	147	157	167	177	187	197
8	18	28	38	48	58	68	78	88	98	108	118	128	138	148	158	168	178	188	198
9	19	29	39	49	59	69	79	89	99	109	119	129	139	149	159	169	179	189	199
10	20	30	40	50	60	70	80	90	100	110	120	130	140	150	160	170	180	190	200